SET YOUR BOOK FREE!

Hello Stranger!

You've caught a travelling book. I'm a very special book. You see, I'm travelling around the world making new friends. I hope I've made another friend in you.

Please go to: www.bookcrossing.com and enter my BCID number. You will discover where I've been and who has read me, and can let them know I'm safe here in your hands. Then...
READ and RELEASE me!

BCID: _____

Registered by: _____

Where: _____

When: _____

RAIDERS OF THE SEVENTH PLANET

A catalogue record for this book is available from the British Library.

ISBN: 978-1-910910-08-5

1st Edition

Indie Authors Press policy is to use paper that are natural, renewable, and recyclable products and made from wood grown in sustainable forests. The logging and manufacturing processes are expected to conform to the environmental regulations of the country of origin.

London | Chile | USA

ACKNOWLEDGMENTS

To Joan, who introduced me to David L.;
To David L. with whom the thing began;
And to Roy, with whom the thing gelled.

DEDICATION

For Roy.

INTRODUCTION

BACK IN THE DAY, Gustavus Adolphus College in Southern Minnesota had a *January Term*, in which students were encouraged to stretch their wings, I developed and taught a one-month class, *Sherlock! Studies in Detective Fiction*. Joan, a good friend whose last name has escaped me, introduced me to her friend, David R. Leslie, visiting from another college for J-Term; like me an aspiring writer of the fantastic, like me, then under the thrall of the Harvard Lampoon's *Bored of the Rings*. We decided to collaborate on a novel of our own, epic in scope and a mite silly.

Together, David and I worked out a plot and drew up a cool map of the Seventh Planet region known as Part of Upper Uranus. We would sit in the canteen over our respective cups of coffee, one of us writing furiously while the other watched. Then the scribbler passed what he'd done to the watcher, who gleefully dismantled what his collaborator had just created and added new complications.

The end of January Term approached. I pledged that I would write about 15 pages, then mail it to David, who would read it, write about 15 pages more, and send it to me. I sent him 15. He didn't send 15 back. I stopped grumbling and set out to finish the thing myself. On March 31 I arrived at a complete draft in a burst of energy that still impresses me. Over the Spring, I wrote a clean-up draft, then sent it to a bunch of publishers. They all rejected it, though one publisher sent a special form saying that, by now, several members of their staff had read the book, but it just wasn't right for them. (Aspiring writers, take note: if you get a note like that it means the editor/publisher sees merit in your work and wants you to keep writing.) Eventually, I set the book aside, looking wistfully at it from time to time. I knew it needed fixing, but I didn't know how to fix it.

Time passed. My friend, novelist/short story writer/f/playwright/essayist/poet/screenplay doctor Roy C. Booth, said, "Say, Eric, do you have any trunk novels?"

I replied, "Three of them, actually, but there's one in particular that would benefit from a new pair of eyes." I handed it to Roy. He saw enough promise in it to try a new draft of his own.

Roy, an experienced collaborator, believes that collaboration should be "seamless." I know that he took out about 10,000 of David's and my words and put in about 15,000 of his own, but apart from a few very specifically topical references I couldn't tell what he'd changed. I do remember that he gently broke it to me that I couldn't call the novel *Up Uranus*! I eventually hit on *Raiders of the Seventh Planet*, which worked for both of us.

Reading Roy's draft, the story became fluid for me again. Roy pointed out to me that there have been a few technological changes since the novel went through its first draft. I updated some of the tech, while deliberately weaving in some more retro. I like retro. I kept a bunch of stuff that was outrageous, while losing some bits that were mean without being especially funny. And a few new scenes floated into my consciousness that could advance the plot while knitting other scenes together. Then Roy added a few bits to my new draft, and I added a couple of bits to that. And— voila!—we arrived at something that we were and are happy to sign our names to.

I hope it makes you laugh.

Eric M. Heideman
June 15, 2016

CHAPTER ONE

IT WAS A BRIGHT, cold day on the planet Uranus. The upper atmospheric temperature hovered around -300 degrees F, a perfect day for the annual Us all ages ski trip and weekend retreat. People eagerly boarded the steed train, clattering equipment, and chattering up a storm. Doleful stay-at-home mothers gave out last minute instructions and saged words of advice.

"Remember, Filbert, honey, dear, that if you kiss an unwed woman your upper lip will fall off. Fool around with the chaperone's if you cannot control yourself."

"Moooooooooom...." Filbert protested.

She patted the tow-headed former urchin on the head. "There, that's a good boy."

The teens were impatient. Very impatient. And they all knew that your upper lip would not fall off, under any ordinary rational circumstances, especially by means of reaching first base. The second idea, however, didn't sound too bad, especially in regards to Miss Jill (more on her later). She was hot! The teen girls and boys dressed against the potential chill in separate units, mostly due to their belonging to good Protestant families.

Finally, they were all in one of the units of the steed train that would take them along Route 66 from Us through Perfect Ambush Pass to the designated ski slopes. To pass the semi-tedious time the senior citizens played bingo, and the younger adults played 20 questions while the teens and kids gorged on cookies and milk and got to know one another better through sing-alongs, pantomimes, and interpretive dance. Jill the chaperone (see, and it *is* later …) looked out her window and thought something. The others nearby stared at her. Wasn't she having any fun?

Time passed.

MEANWHILE, A HUGE SPACESHIP from Earth closely approached its x-urban neighbor, the planet Uranus. The crew, some 7,000 strong, received an audio-directive: "Your attention, crew. Everyone who can be spared from their tasks must make like a tree does to the ship's auditorium."

Upon doing so, the crew looked at the stage upon which stood the Captain and a bewhiskered man with horn-rims whose clothes didn't match.

"Good morning, crew," the Captain said. "We'll be arriving at our destination in a little over an hour. We had been hoping to prep you with a talk by our Ship's Science Officer, but he called in sick, so we've called in our Substitute Science Officer. Let's have a warm welcome for Sub-Science Officer Aaron Hinckley."

Silence reigned through the auditorium. Far in the back, someone coughed twice.

"Good morn—" Mr. Hinckley adjusted the microphone. "Morning. As some of you will recall from astronomy class, Uranus, the seventh planet from our sun, Sol, was discovered in 1781 by musician and amateur astronomer William Herschel. It was the first planetary 'wanderer' not known from ancient times. Uranus, a Roman god, was father to Saturn, who in turn was father to Jupiter, the king of the gods.

The planet Uranus is almost two billion miles farther out from the sun than Earth, a distance which, as you will recall, we have just spent twenty-seven months traversing. Uranus, along with its outer-solar system neighbors, Jupiter, Saturn, and

Neptune, is a 'gas giant'—consisting of a thin gaseous outer layer, a liquid middle layer containing a heady mix of hydrogen, helium, methane, and—lucky for us!—a certain amount of water and a dense rocky inner layer. Some scientists have speculated that it doesn't have the two inner layers, simply consisting of a ball of gas that gets increasingly dense as one approaches its center. Imagine that, folks: a ball of gas big enough to hold 16 Earths." Sub-Science Officer Aaron Hinckley grinned. "We're about to prove that those scientists are full of gas themselves!" He chuckled to himself against a background of silence. He continued, "Uranus has lots of moons—we used to think there were five, but we keep finding more—and several sets of rings though they aren't as big as Saturn's. An eccentric planet, Uranus rotates sideways compared to the Solar System's other worlds'—"

A voice from a middle row called out, "Is there life on Uranus?"

"We think so. That's why we're here. Gravity is 91 percent of Earth-normal, which should put a spring in your step. The examples of Australia, New Zealand, Mars, Venus, and Europa show that life can develop very differently when evolving in an isolated locale. But the Allen-Garrick Parallel-Earth adventures teach us that a world in many ways very different from our own can bear striking similarities. Coincidence...?" Mr. Hinckley ducked as a single paper airplane, then another, then a cascade of planes and spitballs landed near him. Hinckley tipped an imaginary hat and ran offstage.

THE WIND SHRIEKED THROUGH the Krancky Mountains. Genghis Twerp looked down from his strategically sound, rugged mountain pass upon the multi-hued organic steed train passing underneath. An idea slipped into his wrinkled barbaric mind. *Rake*, he thought. He lifted his bone horn and aimed at the lead steed.

Jill Pickswillgoorangestrugiss was now in the back row of

the bus humping Peney Smith, a fellow chaperone under a tarp beneath the gray moons of Uranus.

"Oh, Pickswillgorangy *(her nickname)!*" he shrieked. You are so forceful! Are you having fun yet?"

All Jill Pickswillgoorangestrugiss could manage to say was, "Uhh, uhh, uhhh...."

Suddenly the shrill shriek of a bone horn cut through the silent cooling air! A boulder caught the lead steed squarely in the chest, causing it to jerk free from the steed coupling, and roll into a ditch. *(But no animals were harmed in the composition of this novel.)* The hole in the juncture between steeds hissed with escaping air and screaming senior citizens. Moved by these panicky noises, the remaining steeds rearranged the train into a circle.

Genghis Twerp then unleashed his barbaric horde of slavering unhygienic Munjii. They leaped from the surrounding hilltops—which were craggy and rugged, warmed by the distant but radiant orb of the sun from which did they but know it a strange menace was about to descend upon their peaceful yet rustic planet—brandishing their gleaming silver swords and drooling with blood lust.

In the bus, Jill Pickswillgoorangestrugiss was finally satisfied. Unfortunately, Peney, overstimulated by pitching woo and by the steed crash up ahead, lay comatose. Jill Pickswillgoorangestrugiss took charge of the situation by pulling from Peney's pants a pocket watch and hurling it at the lead Munj, striking him about the head and shoulders, causing his upper torso to separate partially from his body and his dandruff problem to cease immediately forthwith. But the Munjii as a collective whole were not fazed. They retreated to a distance of about thirty yards and began to hurl insults with piercing reckless abandon.

"Presbyterians eat snuff!" shouted the largest and fiercest looking Munj.

"The Munjii are Fungii," the teens and kids chanted back.

"The Munjii are Fungii! The Munjii are Fungii! The Munjii are Fungii! The Munjii are Fungii! The Munjii are Fungii! The Munjii are Fungii! The Munjii are Fungii! The Munjii are Fungii! The Munjii are Fungii!"

"Your mothers bake lousy cornbread!" shouted a smaller, more surreptitious Munj.

Now the non-voting age potential skiers were outraged, livid even. They dug into their lunch pails and threw tomatoes, screaming, "Munjes eat sponges! Munjes eat sponges! Munjes eat sponges! Munjes eat sponges!"

GENGHIS TWERP STOOD UPON the hilltop and surveyed the battle. *Yeah,* he thought, *this is pretty good plunder, yup, yup.*

But it's time for these softening up tactics to end. He sent for his most trusted messenger, a hunch-backed, sloth-eyed sadist with an equally bad complexion named Frank.

"Yes, boss?" asked Frank. "What can I do for you? Hmm?"

"Frank, quite frankly I don't like the way our troops are hanging back, by Crod. Don't they know that the bus is manned by midgets? They're trying to sneak their gold through to the ski slopes," said Genghis Twerp, knowing how the Munjii hated midgets and loved gleaming gold.

Frank bolted down the ski hill screaming. "They're not kids; they're midgets! They're midgets! And they're hoarding gold! Hoarding! Aaaahhhhggghhh!" Beneath the chortling eyes of Genghis Twerp, the enraged Munjii charged headlong (literally) at the bus.

Already weakened by the ninety-minute barrage of insults, the teens looked in dismay to Jill, who alone among them still maintained a cool exterior. Jill Pickswillgoorangestrugiss looked back, thinking... *What the hell am I supposed to do?*

The schnussball coach elbowed her way into the teens' organic train compartment. "Jill," she said, "the kids are worn out from all the name calling and bullying by those nasty Munjes. You've got to get them to safety!"

Jill shrugged. "It's not like I'm unwilling. I'm just fresh out of ideas."

The coach scowled at Jill. "I thought you majored in planetary science in college? Surely you remember that our planet rotates sideways in relation to our solar system's other worlds. In times of extreme stress, it is possible to access that sideways energy, especially when compounded with the special energy generated by minors, to open a sort of doorway to ...somewhere else."

Jill said, "Yeah, I remember reading about that, but it struck me as pretty theoretical."

The coach shrugged in return. "Can you think of a better time to test the theory?"

Working in tandem, Jill and the coach vacated the kids and teens—and the still-sleeping Peney, whom Jill carried with an arm under his shoulder—from the steed train, and gathered them in a small clump of land within the steed train's protective circle. The coach and Jill began singing and clapping their hands to old Rockerfella camp songs. One by one, the young people woke up— finally, even Peney—and joined in, singing, dancing, clapping, shouting, to the background noise of Munjii, reaving (or were they just raving?) and screaming, coming ever closer.

Then a door did open in the air, and a cyclone descended upon them, and an armada of eagles dove to carry the kids away. The soundtrack rose to operatic levels, as the sky got really bright. Then, as quickly as it takes to tell, the sound and light and wind ceased. The kids went on to another level of adventures, which this novel may or may not get around to chronicling. Maybe. Possibly. We'll see.

The coach brushed a tear out of her eye. "Good luck, kids."

Then the Munjii reached the steed train, and the slaughter began.

6

Suddenly, the sky of Uranus was lit by much light. Metallic objects were descending slowly through layers of the semi-liquid atmosphere, armed to the teeth with heat weapons and terrifying insignia. Eagerly, the enormous crew of space-happy Earthlings looked from portholes and over the gun sights.

"No oil wells?" inquired the Captain, blinking.

The Captain of this crew thought, *my mother always wanted me, even before I was born, to be the first man on Uranus. Now I almost am, hahahahahahahahahahaha!*

The first mate was Republican. His grandfather voted for David Eisenhower in 2028 on the Neo-Recloned-Nixonian ticket. He wanted a free and clear monopoly and power from Uranus...and true love. He owned the finest horse on Venus.

No oil wells? thought the first mate. *No native dancing girls in their primitive splendor? Oh, dear. What a letdown. Nertz.*

"In one respect, at least, the Uranians are a happy people," said the Chaplain, wisely.

"Why?" asked a passing crewman.

"They have no lawyers," he replied.

Security Chief Alf Simpson was the military adviser for the entire Fleet. He looked through spectroscope, through horoscope for signs of civilization. *Where is everybody?*

"Ensign Pulverize, get on the loudspeakers. I want to deliver an ultimatum."

"Sir."

"On the double, Ensign."

"Sir, the loudspeakers are not designed to function in liquid air. Besides, who do we deliver—"

"I gave an order, Ensign," growled Security Chief Alf Simpson. "My horoscope informs me that a large, warlike civilization with hundreds of years of proud tradition exists in the Krancky Mountains."

"Say what?" interjected Ensign Pulverize. Security Chief Alf

Simpson fires his blaster, sending the Ensign to the netherworld.

The ship's Private First Class was named Capped Anthony Spaulding. He had just spent nine weeks exploring in Africa, where a mishap in a fabulous lost city gave him split hemispheres, before he accepted this assignment. He thought, *Fuck this shee it. Why am I ridin' in this here ship? What's in it for me?* Capped Anthony Spaulding was French. He hungered for the body of some totally alien creature, preferably one shaped like an octopus, for he felt that if his consciousness were indeed placed within such a beast, he would achieve total unity of body, mind, and soul—Nirvana.

There were seven thousand people in the Earth crew. All of them were force-fed black dex until they couldn't see straight. They did not sleep or repress their fantasies. In other words, the order of the ship is based directly on the fact that the crew is nuts. It was the only way they could get them to go. Remember, most of these men played college football. The Captain at one time dreamt of leading Notre Dame to a national championship. *(This part was crummy, so we X'd it out. You're welcome. — Da Authors)*

"Captain, sir, there's a battle coming in on the telescope. Reaving barbarians in the Perfect Ambush Pass are doing extreme and irreparable lethal harm to unarmed civilians."

"Thanks, Mate. We'll fix that on the spot." The Captain grabbed the loudspeaker herself and shouted, "Now cut that out, you guys! Quit wiping out those civilians or we'll kick your collective ass."

The coach heaved a sigh of relief. Each Munj was eager to cooperate with this vast, gleaming metal object that talks from out the sky. They backed up a discreet distance from the bus.

"They're discreetly far from the bus," the Captain said. "We can wipe 'em without striking the civilians. Hit them lasers."

Within seconds, all of the Munjii (except Frank, of course) were moldering mounds of meat. Only Genghis Twerp remained, hiding face down on the mountain pass, super-scared.

"Pilot, prepare to land," the Captain said, triumph mounting in her voice. "Ground crew, prepare to greet the natives, you know how."

The ship lowered to the surface of Uranus, not two hundred yards from the rejoicing Us picnickers. The picnickers all wave excitedly. It is even bigger than the UFO books said it would be.

Six thousand nine hundred eighty Earthmen run down the ship's landing, Gatling guns blazing. The weather, while cold, was not unbearable, because of the humidity.

Soon the Us weekend party members are all dead.

"Which way to your leader man?" Capped Anthony Spaulding asked.

The coach raised a stiffening arm and pointed down Route 66 in the direction of Us.

***

CHAPTER TWO

MEANWHILE, IN HIS PALACE at Antwerp, the Big King Twerp, sees all, hears all. In his palace at Antwerp, the Big King Twerp makes his plans for complete domination of Part of Upper Uranus. He horns, "Honey; honey lasts a long time, a long time, mmummumm, a long time."

His servant, an illiterate escapee from Edgar R. Burroughs's (1875-1950, American fantasy-adventure writer) Barsoom, asks, "Is the plans ready yet, sire?"

"Shut up, son." With these words a foundling in the Krancky Mountains was sent down the ski slopes on a reed raft, weeping for his mother who is smiling beatifically at the sky which peeks through a small barred window at the top of her cell in the Big King Twerp Asylum for Annoying Virgin Mothers.

It was raining.

✳✳✳

CHAPTER THREE

MEANWHILE, IN HIS PALACE at Antwerp, the Big King Twerp answered a telephone call.

"Hello?" he inquired, breathless from running up the sixteen flights of narrow cold, steps that lead to the top of the Telephone Tower.

"Is this the Big King Twerp?" asked the mysterious voice on the other end of the line.

"No, it's Lenny's Laundry,"replied Big King Twerp, perplexed, who had been answering such nonsense on his private line for well over two years now.

"Hey, why don't you go take a walk?"

"Oh, yeah? Well, same to you, buddy. Up yours."

"Think you're pretty funny, huh?"

"Not as funny as your face." Big King Twerp allowed himself a smile. *Now that one was downright clever*, he thought.

"Hey, pal, I got friends."

"Well, thanks for calling, anyway." Big King Twerp hung up. "These crank calls from the Krancky Mountains have got to stop. No, seriously. Things will be different when I'm King of all of Part of Upper Uranus," he said, out loud to no one in particular, trudging slowly down sixteen flights of cold, narrow stairs.

At the bottom, he met his servant, Ish, a D'Wharf, who was returning from the Land of Thug with news of the Thugs.

"What's new?" asked the Big King Twerp.

"The harrying of the Pass has stopped, and the Twerps of the Pit are itching and raring."

"What?" asked Big King Twerp.

"Somebody in Gnorway caught a forty-pound carp, and the High Steppers lost nine to six."

"What?" said Big King Twerp. "Darn, I had a ten spot riding on that game."

"The Ugly Thugs are gathering for a convention on the shores of the Sea Ontheskale."

"Good, soon all will be ready," Big King Twerp said, pulling out a map of Part of Upper Uranus. *(Due to budget concerns and whatnot, there be no map in this here book. Let the readers figure it out!—Da Editor.)*

"Soon will I bring harmony to the whole of this rustic yet backward land. From the Sea Ontheskale in the southwest to Gnorway in the east, nothing but a slag heap will remain." A feral light entered his eyes. "Only *Genghis Twerp* can flinch my plans to *conquer the universe!*" he screamed, putting his fist through his steel table.

Big King Twerp, who was a short, round-hipped but handsome man with steaming gray hair, ruddy lips and pointed, but cleft chin—full of memories of childhood (he came from a poor but noble family of Twerps that were not known for being particularly polite, or bright, for that matter) when he had leaped carefree up and down the walls of the Great Fissure only to grow into a morbid worried youth searching for knowledge of the world beyond until one day out of a supply truck there dropped the only television set west of the Weird Marsh (oh, how he had rejoiced! Oh, how he had set his cunning mind to work for the thing he had always lacked—power!) until now he ruled all the Twerps and his influence extended even into the land of the Thugs; but it was not enough; still he was dissatisfied—turned to Ish and said, "I want you to go back to the Thugs and tell them to move to the East and take care of Them. After that, take care of the ship."

Above the palace, the sun glowed warmly, but it looked like it would rain. Suddenly, the telephone rang.

Big King Twerp sighed and started to head up the steps.

**

CHAPTER FOUR

"THAT WAY TO US!" shouted Capped Anthony Spaulding.

"Who cares?!" responded the crew.

"I wonder if there are any oil wells in Us?"

"If there are, Captain, I recommend that we march there at once and level the place."

"Shouldn't we go there in the ship? It's faster, and besides, high heels are murder to march in."

"No, Captain," interjected Security Chief Alf Simpson. "They'll be expecting that. We should go overland and take them by surprise."

"Good thinking, Security Chief Alf Simpson. When we get back to Earth (if, actually) I'll recommend you for promotion."

They left Fritz, the engineering man, to guard the ship, and proceeded in a southerly direction on Route 66 towards Us.

CAPTAIN'S LOG (WRITTEN BY 1st Mate):

April 1st, 22:55. *We were marching along Route 66 when a small object on the side of the road caught our attention. It was a blue sapphire plant, probably the only one of its kind in the Solar System. We picked it and went on.*

23:15. We came to the outskirts of Us. We walked through the peaceful but modern streets unopposed. Occasionally people would wander out of their houses or shops, so we shot them. We encountered no real resistance until we reached the police station. There a fierce battle ensued. The fortress's thick brick walls featured small windows from which a man could fire without fear of being shot himself. After an hour of unending rifle and machine gun fire, the police still put up a stiff resistance. It only ended when, after showing great bravery, the men of the first heavy artillery battery were able to wheel their two 12' ("Big Bart") howitzers to within 100 yards of the station and plaster it with armor piercing shells.

00:30. At great risk to his life, Security Chief Alf Simpson officially ended the battle by stepping through the brick powder of the devastated structure and asking several of the mortally wounded defenders for their impressions of the fray for the crew newsletter. The Captain issued orders for the crew to form patrols and search out and destroy any remaining enemy soldiers. The crew scattered, destined to be busy for several hour.

CAPTAIN'S LOG, APRIL 4ᵗʰ, 00:00. (Written by Security Chief Alf Simpson). Uh, the main inceedint too rahport a the last phew days is the inseabordanation of Jon Trahwler, who iz nothin but a maker truble. Are patrol wuz serching the sothern sextor of south Us for bad guys. We're goin threw house by house one at a time doin the duty. I mean we kill the enemy. But first we read them there rights. We observe the geneva convenshun. Never let it be said a army boy aint a good boy.

But this Trahwler fella he's all mad over this. He wants to let everyone go, says theyr not troops just sivilyuns. We've heard that one before. And the prisoners they keep saying just wait you guys will get yours. You just killed the police but we got an army wating for you. So I always ask them, ware is it then and they can never tell me they just say wayt around fatty they'll find you. Well I cant stand that so I shoot 'em. I think they must be the army themselvs or else we'd see them somware else.

15

But Trahwler, he says (Quote) Fools. Idiots! Is this what we came to Uranus to do? We're ravaging Uranian ecology and making hash of the indigenous population. Why can't we offer their civilization the benefits of our technology without imposing our own wasteful standard of living on them? Can't peace and justice cross the borders of interstellar space? Aren't we all brothers and sisters in our maker's eyes?

So I say back that you cant teech an old dog new tricks and you can't make no omlets if you don't break no eggs. Besides, houses make good cover.

I tells 'em that I used to know a woman that cud shoot as good as me so how do I know these womin dont got guns or maybe they can run off in the hills and shoot at stragglers? I say to him how do you know that, huh, how do you know that? I tell him that corporals should sit and think with there mouths shut so they can watch there sgts. And maybe sum day he'll be as good as them. But he tells me I'm no sgt. So I tell him that's true I'm his sgts boss. So he better stop winging are men when he finds them havin a little fun with the prisoners. Anyway if he does it he should have fun himself instead he lets them get away. But he wudn't lissen he gives a big speech

We can build this land—make it grow! We can grow crops where now there is devastation, and we can end these poor people's dire poverty. Remember how we re-cloned the Martian mummies and helped restore their cheerful, advanced civilization? Should space explorers cease their benevolence just because the Democrats are out of office? Let us cross the singing borders of space to seek to strive, to find, and not to yield.

A little rud haired kid whud ben listning aplauded him which I wanted to shoot him but Trawler woulda stoped me so I threw the kid in the brig.

Things are going real good otherwise.

THE NEXT DAY, APRIL 5th, the Captain called the crew together. Flanked by Security Chief Alf Simpson and an honor guard of sixty heavily armed commandos, the Captain spoke to them from behind a bulletproof plexiglass podium. "I know you men are tired," she said with a coquettish grin, "And you certainly deserve to be. Nevertheless, the time has come when we must move on. We are the best thing that has happened to this planet since the current inhabitants crawled out of the slime. We owe it to Uranus not to limit the blessing of our presence to this one small hamlet. As one survivor of the recent battle said to me the other day, 'It could be worse.' We must spread this feeling of optimism across the globe. We must let it multiply until there is not a person quivering in any dark corner on Uranus who does not have this feeling."

Suddenly, from somewhere in the massed crew, someone yelled, "Hey, buddy, go take a swimsuit!" Immediately the massed firepower of the honor guard replied. As the dead and wounded were carried away, the Captain continued.

"This reminds me of the time when I was a small child in the Ozarks and my father took me fishing, which he was often wont to do due to his upbringing and folksy-like ways and temperament. It was a hot summer day. One of those days when your clothes stuck to your chest and back. Sweaty. Humid. We were very uncomfortable. All day we sat out in the hot sun in our little open boat. The people in the boat next to ours had forgotten to bring their hats. Late in the afternoon, one of them fell over, exhausted. Neither they nor we caught any fish."

"I wonder what she's getting at," whispered Joel McKray to his buddy brother Brad McKray.

"She's getting at her Oedipus complex."

"How do you figure that?"

"Obviously, she wanted to kill him instead of going fishing."

"Ah. Good point."

"Do you think the Captain is keeping the food to herself?"

"She sure isn't keeping the dex to herself."

"They seem to be getting bigger every day."

"So does the Captain."

"Look at that enormous orange and green condor sitting on the telephone pole!"

"Where? Where?"

"Just kidding," Brad McKray said, giving Joel McKray a hard slap on the back. Both turned their attention once again to the speech. They hadn't missed anything.

"So that's the plan," the Captain was saying. "I'm sure that if we all adhere to it carefully, to the letter, proverbial or otherwise, we shall conquer. We shall persevere."

The crew cheered wildly.

With gusto and spirit and much ado, they marched to the border of Us/Them to look for and lay waste the Us army. (Them could wait.) Upon arriving at the border, they found an elaborate work of earth and concrete and steel. Fortunately, the bunkers and trench work were designed to face an attack from the opposite direction. It was devoid of life. "My, my," the Captain said, fluttering his perplexed eyelash. "They're not there."

"In the castle, cuz," Capped Anthony Spaulding said. "They're afraid to come out and meet us."

"Good point, Private First Class," the Captain said. "What do you make of the situation, Simpson? You're the military adviser."

"Beats me," replied the clever but bloodthirsty fellow.

"Do not attack!" implored John Trawler in a loud but gentle voice. "Send a deputation waving the white flag of peace. Perhaps they will share with us their secrets, their culture, and their ways of living in light and harmony."

"Who's this nut?" asked the Captain.

Security Chief Alf Simpson stepped forward and said, "This man has been giving us a lot of trouble lately. I recommend that we execute him immediately. I suggest we toss him into a big gunny sack with a pair of rabid inbred wolverines."

"Nah," said the Captain, running her eyes up and down John Trawler's lithe, sinuous, firmly muscled body. "We'll give him another chance. Mercy is as mercy does."

Security Chief Alf Simpson coughed into his hand. "Bullshit."

"What was that, Security Chief Alf Simpson? I didn't quite catch that," said the Captain.

"But he's bad for the morale of the troops."

"Who cares?" With that, the argument ended.

A clever idea came to Security Chief Alf Simpson. "Say There, Sarge," Capped Anthony Spaulding said. "Why don' you send *him* up to that there castle with a white flag while the Captain ain't lookin'?"

"For a Private First Class, Capped Anthony Spaulding, you ain't too stupid."

"Thanks, Sarge."

Capped Anthony Spaulding leaped at the Captain yelling, "Look out Captain, the shit hit the fan!"

Meanwhile, Security Chief Alf Simpson was talking quietly to John Trawler. "Look, John Trawler, you're probably right. We should at least give them a chance to surrender before we slash them to pieces. I give you my permission to try to talk some sense into them."

John Trawler's beard leaped with joy! With vindication! If only one is persistent, all doors will open to him! To think that this boor, this professional ape, had the pure light of reason flash through his brain! Anything was possible!

Ripping a white blouse from the ship's laundry, John Trawler quickly fashioned a crude but ingenious flag of whiteness.

19

His heart pounding, he set across the coverless space between the crew and the castle.

Quick as the quick brown fox, Security Chief Alf Simpson was over to the artillery officer. "Unlimber those guns!" he barked. "Get a fix on that there castle!"

"Sure, clever but bloodthirsty, sir. Your wish is our wish, your friends are our friends, and those you wish to destroy, we shall destroy." (The battery commander was a recent graduate from law school.) "Hey, Heinlein, line up that castle over on the right there, okay, fella?"

Several artillerymen, stripped to the waist and sweating, sauntered over to the guns. Heinlein squinted at the castle through an ancient sextant. "It's hard to see the thing through this blasted fog."

"The Captain should ration the dex a little more carefully; I think, sir."

"You may have a point," said Spaulding, blinking.

"Capped Anthony Spaulding, you devil!" squealed the Captain.

"Sorry, sir, I didn't mean...I mean, the artillery and with the shootin' I thought—"

"Shooting? Security Chief Alf Simpson, what's this about shooting?"

"Wait! I see some movement! A white flag!" (Heinlein)

"What *is* this man prattling about, Security Chief Alf Simpson?"

"It's the enemy, sir. They raised the white flag and then started firing!

"Unscrupulous bastards! Slobbering sock puppets! Demonizing Democrats!"

"I've had the howitzers unlimbered, sir."

"Good thinking, Security Chief Alf Simpson. H.Q. knew what they were doing when they insisted that we bring along an experienced military man."

"The dex weren't no bad idea, neither," said Capped Anthony Spaulding, interjecting.

"Shut up, Private." The Captain slapped Security Chief Alf Simpson soundly on the back. "Howitzers, fire at will!"

The great gaping mouths of the howitzers began to spit gobs upon gobs of death over the castle and onto the surrounding plain. Tongues of fire licked at the castle walls. The troops cheered. They capered and danced about, sticking out their dried tongues, and making all sorts of rude faces.

"Nah Nah Na Nah Nah, can't hit me can't hit me!" they jeered.

"Cease fire!" ordered the Captain. "First Battalion! Fix bayonets!"

"Wait, Captain, I don't think that would be a good idea." Security Chief Alf Simpson cocked an eyebrow for emphasis.

"Why not? I haven't ever seen a bayonet charge?"

"Well, sir, the castle's still on fire. If we go charging into it, someone is likely to get hurt. Burned even."

"Damn," the Captain said, pouting and stamping her little foot.

"I'm sorry, sir, but that's just how it is."

"I don't care! I don't care! I order those men to charge, and I'll court martial anyone who tries to stop me."

"I have an idea, Captain."

"Yes, Security Chief Alf Simpson?" She tried an authoritative smile for the toadeater. It didn't work exactly as she had hoped.

"Let's cross the border into Them. We can charge *their* stone wall. It's just as good as any old castle," wheedled Security Chief Alf Simpson, now spinning his right hand in a circular motion for even more emphasis.

The Captain sniffed. "Oh, I suppose so. But never ever

question my orders again." The Captain stamped her tiny foot, her arms akimbo.

"Right, sir," the sly Security Chief Alf Simpson responded.

A great fire enveloped the castle, gutting, searing, ashening all it could burn. Smoke unfurled high into the air like a black flag, like unto a devil's chimney. Paralyzed by the fumes, insects dropped like flies, spiraling to their dooms. Crumpled in the narrow furrow left by a plow (the only thing that had saved him), John Trawler lay dazed and glazed while the hot flaming fire unsympathetically burned its way towards him.

The Earthmen marched towards the Them barricades which had stood for centuries, which Us had never penetrated during all the years of that bloody feud, but which the Earthmen knew they could overcome, if only by their ancient reinforced ideals of manifest destiny and downright persnickety perseverance. However, they did not know what only the now unconscious John Trawler knew, that the castle had been empty all along!

Will John Trawler survive? Will he be able to warn his companions of their imminent peril and possible impending doom? You certainly won't find out in...

***

CHAPTER FIVE

THIRTY-FIVE YEARS BEFORE the principle events in this tale, two brothers played in the ginormous sandbox in the noble families' daycare center near the great Court of Antwerp. Seven-year-old Son-of-the-Duke Twerp had constructed a fort out of sand. Owing to the chemical properties of his world of Uranus, the sand, like putty, could be molded into any shape, but, once the Prince poured liquid helium over his structure, it froze into the durability of rock. Son-of-the-Duke Twerp smiled upon his work. "Let's see you storm *this* fort, little brother."

Son-of-the-Duke Twerp's half-brother Genji, though only five years of age, hardly counted as a "little" brother. His naturally athletic frame, enhanced by long summer days running, climbing, playing, and hunting, had taken on the appearance of a healthy lad of eight or nine. As his elder half-brother had worked up his elaborate play castle, young Genji had been lining up hundreds of toy soldiers, at the front of whose ranks stood many troops carrying ladders. Taking his half-brother's invitation, Genji moved the ladders and ladder-carriers up against the fortress walls.

"Take *that!*" cried Prince Twerp, quickly moving from toy cannon to toy cannon along the walls, firing ammonia pellets that swept the ladders backward, collapsing upon ranks and rows of invading soldiers.

"Curses upon you!" yelled G. Twerp, battering the walls of

Son-of-the-Duke Twerp's castle with powerful fists. These walls had been designed to withstand repeated heavy assault, but G. Twerp knew just how to hit. The frozen walls shattered.

Son-of-the-Duke Twerp burst into cascades of sobbing, drawing the attention of a napping Noble Nanny, who escorted G. Twerp outside for a time-out. When they had exited the Noble Daycare Center, the Noble Nanny said, "Off with you, then. Play by the stream for half an hour, then return to beseech your brother's pardon." As the lad ran off, she was unable to repress a smirk, for, truth to tell, she admired his spirit.

G. TWERP CREPT FURTIVELY along the stream bank, peering through the willows at an imaginary enemy who his imaginary band of reavers could surprise. So intent was he on this play that he didn't overhear the stealthy pair of men creeping upon him from behind. More quickly than it takes to tell, one of the men scooped up the lad and placed him upon a steed, then ascended the steed behind him. "Take your hands off my noble person!" he shouted, only to have a rag crammed into his mouth. He struggled to escape, but his abductor wrapped an arm around him, immobilizing him.

The other man said, "Hoot, mon. The lad has strength and spirit. He will be a worthy addition to our apprentice warriors." He winked at the Son-of-the-Duke Twerp, accepting the SotD's bribe, a bag of Noble Metal coins. Then the other man leaped upon his steed, and the two abductors galloped away, bearing their consequent abductee.

Soon thereafter the Noble Nanny ventured to the stream bed in search of young G. She found small signs of a struggle, but the abductors were good at their work, and their trail soon disappeared. Though the King himself sent troops searching in all directions, the lad was never found.

***

CHAPTER SIX

MEANWHILE, THIRTY-FIVE YEARS LATER, Ish, humble servant of the Big King Twerp, trekked forth from the pit of Antwerp to do his sublime master's bidding. Shortly after climbing out of the pit, he found himself in the cruddy but torpid land of the Thugs, which was full of hills and roads and Thugs.

"Hey, hey, my, my," he said, "I've never been here before; in fact, never before have I left the fissure of the Twerps. Still and all, what's good for me boss is good for me. Indeed. Heh. Heh."

A Thug reclining pleasantly on the greensward said, "I don't know what ye want up here, stranger, but we don't like strangers here. State yer business, quick and plainly, or die."

For all his uncouth language, Ish took the Thug to be not unfriendly. "You seem a likely fellow," he said. "Tell me how to organize your entire nation into a horde of reaving barbarians ready to storm the battlements of all the rest of Part of Upper Uranus in the service of the mighty and just King of Antwerp."

A glazed look came into the Thug's eyes, a thunderous belch emerged, and he then rolled over onto his large abused stomach.

Ish poked the Thug with a long pointed stick, but he failed to elicit a response. Falling into great despair, Ish pondered his problem. *How was he to accomplish his munificent master's wishes? How was it possible to organize a fierce, disciplined, reliable fighting force in a land full of naturally inclined (and gluttonously lazy, by the looks of it) anarchists? To even mention the word "cooperation" amongst the Thugs was to invite hysteria.* He thought and thought.

Suddenly, he scrambled to the top of a tall but rustic coniferous tree, pulled out a bull bone horn (a Horn of Power, no less), and began to shout, "Dwarves and gold, Dwarves and gold, get 'em while they're hot! Dwarves and gold, get 'em right here! No sweat, no muss, no fuss! Gentlemen, easy money right here! Dwarves and gold! Dwarves and gold!"

Immediately, a small ragtag army of heavily armed (and equally smelly) Thugs gathered at the foot of the tree. A particularly large, swarthy Thug armed with a broken coffee cup stepped up. "How much were you planning to sell these Dwarves for?" he inquired in a voice that sounded like a hysterical wombat gargling with cherry cola soda pop and sand.

"Sell, you ask? Oho! Money changing hands without violence in the land of Thug? Surely you don't think me that dense?" replied Ish. "I merely wanted to inform you that the Dwarves have embarked on a unilateral policy of disarmament. Nobody is guarding the vaults in More-of-Them-by-the-Sea. You can just walk in there and grab whatever you want. By armfuls, even! A short gentleman in glasses will protest, of course, but, unless you are afraid of hurting his eentsy, weensy, widdle feelings, there is really nothing, nothing to stop you."

"You must dink we're pretty stupid in dis disheveled yet rustic land," piped up an older, yet much hairier, Thug, who smelled of apple shavings and cheap turpentine. "No Dwarves wud do nodin liek dat. Gold is the favrit ting there, even more den wimin."

"Of course, I don't think *you're* stupid. Sheesh. Would I come here, allow myself to be surrounded by an invertible horde of unscrupulous, bloodthirsty gold-crazed lunatics such as yourselves and then tell them an obvious pathetic lie unless I was telling the absolute truth?"

"He's got a point there," a small, intelligent-looking Thug, who specialized in murder by poisoned telegram, piped from the rear of the mob, frantically jumping up and down to be seen and heard.

"But then, what if he doesn't?" mused another, stroking at the mass of stubble on his chin. "What if we are pondering the imponderable? A wise man, from a galaxy far, far away once said, and I quote: 'Gold is what everyone yearns for. Pretty in itself, it also enables us to furnish our homes with other things of beauty. And as gold doesn't rust, objects from which it is fashioned retain their beauty throughout eternity, or as near eternity as makes no difference.'"

The other intelligent Thug said, "But what does that have to do with what that foreigner just said?"

The two Thugs looked at each other in puzzlement. At a loss as to how to solve the problem, they put their hands into their pockets and stared up at the trembling Twerp. One of them threw a rock; "Let's stone him to death," he cried.

A club-footed Thug next to him shot him a glance of unconcealed disdain. "Primitive!" he sniggered.

"Well, let's hear something better from you, then, you overstuffed chair." It didn't matter to Ish now if he sounded rude or hostile. He still had his dignity, after all.

"Quite simple, you mindless baboon. Burn down the tree." Now this Thug was quite smug, and crossed his arms for emphasis, gloating at his wit.

"No, let's shoot him, let's shoot him," piped another. "Ka-pow!"

"Why bother?" drawled a lazy-looking Thug sprawled across a mossy boulder. "He probably doesn't have any money."

"That's right," shouted Ish, "killing me would be pointless. I'm broke. I just came here to share ideas with you. Golden ideas.

Of course, I'm not suggesting that you accept them. Certainly not. It's just that I can't cart all that gold away alone."

"If ya can't do it alone, you shudn't bother ta do it," blurted a proverb-loving Thug, as a fellow Thug placed a "Kick me" sign on his back. Other Thugs nearby chortled at this.

"I don't look at it that way," Ish said. "My experience says that you can get a lot more goods for yourself through cooperation and declaring yourself a corporation than through plain individual work. Four Thugs driving a wagon can haul eight times as much gold as one Thug with a wheelbarrow."

This caused another outburst from the big audience who, being naturally anarchistic, hated any mention of working together, or–ugh!–the mere word "work" in any capacity. "Snipe him!" said a bearded Thug, who had survived to the remarkable old age for Thugs of thirty.

"Throw him off a cliff!" said one, which struck all with whimsical amusement since Thug was full only of plains and slowly rolling hills hardly steep enough to twist a knee or a good face plant nosebleed.

Ish listened respectfully to everyone's suggestions, even the incredibly dumb ones, and then said, "I'm going to make you an offer you *can* refuse. But—you won't want to!"

"Oooo!" came a unified chorus.

"Why don't you all destroy me in whatever way you want to!"

As the throng below roared its approval, Ish scrambled to another tree. The Thugs below were so busy clapping each other on the back, screaming so loud that their eyes closed, gathering wood and rocks, sharpening knives, polishing and cleaning firearms, cranking catapults taut, finding pebbles for slings, and so on and so forth almost to the point of ad nauseam that they failed to notice.

"Kill him! Kill him!" cried Ish in his most bloodcurdling battle cry. Instantly, an incredible volley of almost every destructive device known to Thug reduced the tree to ash. The Thugs looked at each other in astonishment.

"I've never seen anything like it," whispered one in awe.

"Quite," whispered back another.

"Good job," said Ish, standing on a particularly perpendicular hilltop behind the Thugs assembled. "You can blow the top off a mountain, but you can't hit one fleet-footed Twerp." He produced a party favor and blew the razz-dazz on it.

"Hey, ya know he shouldn't ought to have done that," said an inconspicuous but unknown Thug. Many other Thugs agreed.

Ish ran expeditiously toward the Fissure of the Twerps, with a horde of savage, unclean, logic impaired Thugs in hot pursuit.

***

CHAPTER SEVEN

IN A COUNTRY CLUB on the beautiful shores of Sea Ontheskale, Celibate, High King of the D'wharfs, was celebrating the six-hundredth anniversary of peace and tranquility in his ethereally earthy domain. He and his court had gathered here to make merry and to drink of the nectar of the rye plant which was grown far beneath the surface by the wondrous splendor of D'wharfen crypto-science. For six hundred years D'wharfs had lived in peace and harmony and, most importantly, justice. The celebration waxed wild. Overcome by emotion, one by one each noble member of the wise and beneficent rose to speak and praise the noble and polite ways of their ancestors.

"Gentlemen," spoke High King Celibate in a clear, clangorous voice, "I propose a toast to our noble and polite ancestors, may we never join them."

Each member of the court tottered gracefully to his or her feet. Swaying with emotion, they joined their silver goblets in salute.

"Yippee! Yay ancestors!" they cried in accordance with their ancient and respected customs.

Gilfgilf, the youngest D'wharf allowed in the country club (because he made astonishingly witty after-dinner speeches, full of noxious jokes about Us-maidens and delicate pastries) rose with his ready eye and said, "Dear brethren, we all know how good we are—"

"Hear! Hear!"

"I'm as good as anybody alive on Uranus, but—"

"Prove it! Har! Har!" This exceedingly witty remark brought guffaws from the still-waking audience.

"And our ancestors were even better. But we must ponder the state of our world sometime soon. A cloud hangs over our noble horizon."

"Indeed, there is," said High King Celibate, pointing to the window. "I think it looks rather like an elephant."

"No, I'd say it looks more like a doggie," said Weiner, his boon companion. "But the fluffy part keeps changing around the edges. Morphing."

"Danger impends," continued Gilfgilf. "Our age-long friendly rivals, Us, have been obliterated. Slobber-knockered. Our other nice foes, Them, are soon to follow. All this caused by a vast, technologically equipped expedition from the third planet, which we call Bip-Citty.

"Soon, my friends, the Bip Peril will reach this very door. We will be decimated and ripped to shreds as we sit. Our women will be spoken to disrespectfully, our cats and dogs will be raped—"

"So, what else is new?"

"As the bearers of civilization on Upper Uranus, it is our noble and polite duty to destroy these dastardly denizens of dour decimation. We must dedicate our dutiful nobility and politeness. I demur."

Although the D'wharfs were a noble and polite, peaceful people, given more to holding a goblet in the graceful curve of their hand than to bludgeoning barbarians, the logic of this statement could not but fail to elude them. The memory of the deeds of their noble and polite ancestors stirred in them thoughts of the good old days when everyone was younger and could hold his nectar without provocation or embarrassment.

"These are grave words," said High King Celibate, "and it is but fitting that we sleep on them. Haste makes waste, as my noble and polite father used to say. Meanwhile, let us remember the happiness of the more graceful times before the opening of the Great Fissure. Waiter, pour me another drink."

At that a tall yet eight-foot Gnorwegian named Siv said, "Ya, sure, I ban serve you good. You like maybe a little coffee with your drink?"

"Good fellow," said High King Celibate, patting him on the knee. "I'll have my coffee *after* my drink if you don't mind. That is if it isn't too much trouble for you." He gave a log cabin smile to the trusted towering servant, blinking.

"Ya, I do that good, boss. You know," he said, leaning over several yards to whisper in Big King Twerp's ear, pointing the while at Gilfgilf, and nodding significantly, a shrewd, satisfied smile on his face, but the old battle-scar suddenly standing out on his ankle like a throbbing vein, "I ban tink it rain putty soon putty hard."

Meanwhile, in a dark corner on a far side of the room, two suspiciously tall characters shrouded in yellow-orange were whispering among themselves. A middle-aged but still feisty D'wharf, moved somewhat to action by Gilfgilf's dire words, sauntered over silently to the light-some pair.

Words drifted to him from beneath the neon cowls of their shrouds. "I think this is going to turn out to be a dud."

"Looks that way," replied his equally neon cowled friend. We fly all the way here from the Tower to watch these oafs talk themselves into oblivion. We should've stayed there and covered the golf tournament."

"That's the trouble," sighed the first. "He doesn't have enough people to cover all the events around here."

"True."

"It would help if we weren't joined at the waist."

32

Paragon listened to this strange conversation. *It bodes ill,* he thought, *no good, bad, evil, ick, yuk. Who are these strange beings?*

"What if the Ambush at Them wipes the Earthers out? We won't even have any story at all."

"On the other hand," said the other, "if they do make it to More of Them by the Sea, we'll have gotten the exclusive story on their last hours of peaceful splendor. Remember, we were so busy covering the coffee-strike that we missed the scoop on Us."

"Ah, true, true."

Paragon, more and more perplexed, fell asleep.

"Listen, you guys," Gilfgilf was saying, "what do I have to do to get you worked up? I mean, you guys are the government. If you won't take defensive action, I'll have to organize a citizen's committee. And we all know what a drag that is. I think I'll just leave town for a while." Gilfgilf fell to mumbling.

"Let's play a game," said High King Celibate. "It's got five hands, and it walks and talks. What is it?"

"A sowboy!" said Siv and broke into laughter. The rest of the noble and polite company chuckled gracefully.

***

CHAPTER EIGHT

GENGHIS TWERP WAS ALONE. Around him lay the vast waste of the Krancky Mountains.

Heck darn, thought Genghis Twerp. *My band has been disbanded. How can I loot and ravage the dank and bleak countryside now? How? How!? Someone is going to pay for this.*

The strange cry of a Uranian mountain bat had dripped through the liquid air. So strong was the force of the wind as it whipped through the mountains that he found he could swim in it. *Beats walking,* he thought. He knew he had to save his strength for the great tussle ahead. The Krancky Mountains were noted for their wildness and for the strange bloodthirsty beasts that wandered about.

There on a craggy peak above him, he saw wandering a strange cranky looking mountain person. "Hey, krancky, what's new?"

"Well," came the reply, "that question certainly isn't." For the people of the Krancky Mountains never gave a straight answer if they could help it.

"Where would be a good place to find a band of bloodthirsty, bleak big barbaric warriors who can bear grudges and take orders?"

With a shriek of laughter, the Krancky person turned into an avalanche crashing towards him.

"Try the forest if you get out of this alive, sucker," said an even-now fading voice.

"Good idea," said Genghis Twerp, dodging nimbly for one so hapless. "The forest is full of fiercely independent, lusty killers. I hear they rob from rich and poor alike." The mighty Twerp marched to the edge of the forest which, since he was right next to it, he got there pretty fast. *(HE'S NOT REALLY NEXT to the forest. We rechecked our map, so we had to cross this section out.— Da Authors.*

P.S. But he still got there, but it took a long time.)

AT NIGHT, HE SHIVERED with fear as fierce mountain bats swooped inches above his erect hair. For all he knew, some cranky person could descend from a craggy peak and throw a rock at him. Why didn't he stay among the Steppes when he had the chance? Nothing ever happened there, and it always seemed so important.

As the limp, pale sun peaked warily over the peaks, Genghis Twerp heard the sound of some creepy thing creeping behind him. He was too scared to move.

"Genghis!" said the ever-familiar voice of Frank, the sloth-eyed hunchback. "Air ye alive?"

"Yeah, and how about you?"

"Pretty good. There's a pain in my heart, though, where the Gatling gun bullets went through."

"Hey, I'm really sorry about all this, verily and truly I am."

"Forget it." Frank shrugged, "It happens."

"What are you doing on the outskirts of the forest?" pressed Genghis Twerp, placing his hands at his manly jutting hip for polite and noble emphasis.

"Same thing as you. Looking for allies to organize a revenge against the cruel people of Planet III, which we call 'The Great Donkey.'"

They embraced and fell to weeping for many minutes over

the very joy of each other. Thus renewed, they began to boast. "By cracky," stormed Genghis Twerp, "these Donklings shall know the full and righteous wrath of my +2 broadsword."

"And the sting of my +1 Stiletto of Insect Slaying," joined Frank.

"If only I could find my +2 broadsword." Genghis Twerp flexed a mightily thewed bicep for added emphasis.

"And I my +1 Stiletto of Insect Slaying," sighed Frank.

"I've never seen you use a stiletto, +1 or otherwise, Frank. You but boast idly. You but boast the breeze." Genghis Twerp removed his hand from his manly jutting hips, still noble, yet no longer polite.

"Nor have you ever held a broadsword in your mighty thews, great Twerp."

"Kreegah!" Enraged, Genghis Twerp sent the driveling Munj sprawling with a single swipe of his sinewy, knuckled fist. Spitting teeth, the short yet broad-nosed Munj rose groggily to his stunted bowed legs, drawing his curved straight razor of masterwork manufacture.

"Wen, no you dun ib," sputtered Frank, wiggling his ears.

"Does this mean our long, loyal liaison is over?" inquired the aghast barbarian warlord, drawing his Colt .45.

"Loog at the bib birb drobbing from abub!"

Genghis Twerp looked up, then heard a sound such as might be made by a short, stocky pervert leaping at him. He lowered his sights swiftly enough to drill Frank four times each through the brain, heart, and groin. Frank fell—in three different directions. "That should make the Kranky sheep happy," he said. "Goodness knows how their masters starve them."

He headed for the Lots of Trees Forest which, and since he was right next to it, it didn't take him long to get there.

That night it got dark, so he built a fire. "Hope they don't mind me burning up their trees, heh, eh." Genghis Twerp, a wise master of woodcraft, fire-making, and oodles of other things besides that which has already been listed, hunched his mightily muscled thews and the wiry- built muscles over the warm yet burning blaze which he had whipped out of two sticks and the nuts from a squirrel nest and the afore referred to by way of squirrel.

A slightly noticeably loud sound echoed from all directions. He collapsed to the ground (severely burning his right knee cap again, just like he did at Little Barbarians Camp decades prior), pulled out his Colt .45 and looked about him, his barbarian instincts now hot and piercing. Seventeen Green Forest Folk with drawn cocked bows were frowning at him, clearly non-plussed by his presence and his disregard for the prevention of forest fires.

"Stand, stranger, or be skewered to the molecules with our sacred mystic Yaka metal tipped arrows from whence ye came in the dawning days when dinosaurs and other assorted creepy crawlies leaped frivolously over the fire-falls and deep dark crevices of despair. Oh, and drop the gun, please."

Genghis Twerp hid the gun in his pants and stood up, slowly. "Uhh, hi there, fellas. What can I do for you?"

"Why come ye here to our darkling abode? Only Green Forest Folk and spiders of enormous size dwell here within this mirky wood. No great-thewed bumbling Plainsmen have we seen since great Mastiff led us on a quest against the evil wizard Jasux, and we hacked the One True Porta-Phone from his nerd pack."

"Aye and verily," confirmed another.

Genghis Twerp now rose to his full height, for more emphasis. "I come here to lead you as Mastiff did long ago. For again we face an evil foe. A cruel race has come among us from the sky. They rape and plunder as most men eat and drink. Death follows them about like an eager puppy.

"I myself have narrowly escaped their tepid wrath. Of my once proud warrior band, only I remain. I am looking for followers to lead on a quest of revenge."

"Our mission with Mastiff brought us not but malady," He of the Green Forest Folk intoned. "Our band was lessened by three score. If we remain in this safe place, we will suffer no harm. Why should we not skewer you on the spot for trying to bring us a skull splitting headache?"

Genghis Twerp spread out his thickly thewed arms for even more emphasis. "These foemen are rich. They have weapons that would make your eyes bug out. Yet they are bumbling mortals, and a stealthy band such as yours and mine could kill them as they kill sleeping babes and small children with Gatling guns (them, they have the guns, not the small children, I mean). And they are laden with plunder taken from the dead. Should we get these things and plumb their dark and terrible secrets, we would be very powerful."

"What proof have we that ye speak true, plainsman? Methinks ye but speak to save your worthless hide."

"I can give you nothing but the word of a northerner. A man of the Steppes never lies."

The Green Forest Folk broke into a chorus of guffaws.

"Ye must give us a break, barbarian. Our gullibility is not what ye think it."

While this conversation had been carried on, some of the Green Forest Folk had crept into the green trees above Genghis. As the spokesman for the Green Forest Folk finished speaking, they dropped a large net over the great thewed man of the Steppes. Seeing Genghis's tall, menacing figure drop thrashing in this entanglement, the Green Forest Folk rushed him.

"Aw, puckernuts, come on, guys," said Genghis Twerp. "That isn't really nice," as they did something to him.

Hours later, when it even was near dawn, Genghis Twerp awoke again, and he was still surrounded by lots of Green Forest Folk but nonetheless worried. A shadowy figure approached. From the silhouette, Genghis guessed it was not a man. When he began to feel long slender tapered fingers run through his long, dark barbaric hair and to smell the eau of perfume, he was even more sure it was not a man. When he felt certain voluptuous charms brush against his cheek, he was even more sure it was not a man.

"You're not a man," he said.

"I'm surprised a brute such as ye be can mark the difference," said a husky female voice from the darkness.

"Indeed, wench," said he, cheered to bravado by the fact that she was indeed in truth, not a man, and this relieved him. "I've *known* many of your kind, if you get my meaning. You're not as soft and cuddly as some, but it looks to me that you'd do."

"Ye talk a good streak, brawny brute," she said, her voice softening somewhat, "but could ye act supply upon it if set free?"

Genghis Twerp knew this type of broad well. Very well. His shoulders, legs, and massive forehead dwarfed the Green Forest Folk in comparison; so she no doubt suspected that his other goodies were proportionately as vast, and wished to test their worth.

"If it's a roll for your money you want, un-net me, and I'll give you a tussle to set you back a week's pay."

"Gee, will you really? Tee hee hee," she said, swiftly unleashing his hands with her short sword.

He crushed her to him with his mighty thews. Her lithe, slender, amphetamine wracked yet voluptuous body writhed in his huge arms, her white alabaster hands pressed tight against his six-pack Jersey Shore abs. *This lass is not unwilling,* he thought, as her lovely fingers slipped beneath his loosely belted pants.

As dawn broke, Genghis Twerp lay on his back next to the woman's temporarily satiated body. He stared into the strange, tree studded landscape of the forest. Above him, the spidery limbs of trees stretched seemingly endlessly upwards. Everywhere were the squirrels with their strange staring eyes. Such a place unnerved a man such as Genghis Twerp, used as he was to the open space of the northern plains and the occasional steppe.

Suddenly, his reverence was broken.

"Hey, this heathen done went and laid Queen Rabid!"

Eight of the Green Forest Folk cried in unison, waving their dainty green fingers at him and making snipping motions for emphasis, "Cut it right off! Cut it right off!" It sounded to Genghis Twerp like part of an old rite, one he would not care to be any part of, real or imagined.

"Ease off, fellas," said the naked, flush-faced woman who, Genghis discerned to his surprise, and some consternation, must be the Green Forest Folks' Queen, "I only got what I asked for. And I'd like to see one of you 'men' treat me that way."

A big, green-clad member of their company began to move forth with a grin but was stayed by the disapproving glances of his fellow Green Forest Folk.

"Uhh, Queen," said a younger, more stolid though blonde one of the green forest men, "our constitution says we gotta be ruled by a virgin Queen Rabid. You ain't no virgin no more, so we gotta kill you and castrate the big fella."

"I be-eth Queen Rabid and the constitution be-eth only oral, so as of this instant, it standeth changed. As of now and forever after, thou all will be ruled by a *non*-virgin Queen, aided on the throne by the most handsome, biggest, brawniest, most virile man of Part of Upper Uranus whom we can get our hands on. *Rrrowr.*" She stuck out her thumb and made a backward thrusting gesture for emphasis. "Consider thyself exiled, kid."

"But..."

She paused for emphasis. "Hit the road, Jack."

"And don't you come back no more, no more!" shouted a chorus of Green Forest Folk, clapping their equally green hands in unison.

"And never come back!" added one particularly gnarled, paler specimen for even more added emphasis.

And thus, did Queen Rabid talk yon youth out of his

objection and sent him packing on his exiled way.

Then she turned to Genghis saying, "This man shall be-eth our champion."

The throng applauded nobly and politely. It could be worse, they thought. Far worse.

Genghis grinned sheepishly. "I owe it all to my mother," he said. "Thanks, Mom," he said, pointing skyward.

Queen Rabid arched an eyebrow. Her smoldering eyes told Genghis that something was wrong.

"Oh," he said with sudden realization, "I didn't mean it that way."

"Genghis," said Queen Rabid, cooing, "as newly appointed champion of the Queen of the Green Forest Folk, it is forbidden for thee to even so much as think of another woman, even thy mother out of whose womb thou were spat out into a dung heap. It is an ancient tradition." And, once again, she and her cohorts made that odd, yet unsettling, snipping gesture for added emphasis.

Genghis Twerp thought, *This could get to be a Thug sheep poop.* But he saw no current alternative that would not lead to a sure and cruel excruciating death. "Sure, baby," he said, "I'm yours for keeps, thine and thine alone, for ever and ever, etc., etc."

"Real good," she said. "We would have much fain been loathe to have to ..." Her silky husky voice trailed off, and a lone tear came into her regal eye, soon it trickled down her face and into her heaving ample bosom.

Hours later, after they had done it again (this time with a bit more passion and far more vocalization) and eaten a hearty, healthy vegetarian lunch, Genghis Twerp (still understandably feeling a bit peckish) said, "Queen Rabid, the only one of your beauteous sex, what about this revenge on the dastardly Earthmen idea? Would it be okay if I led your men to great and lusty battle and showed the craven Donklings who's the boss?"

"Anything thou doth sayest, dear," said she, always having

wanted to be dominated by an awful tough, well thewed, square-jawed, but cute hunk of a man. "But first, let's make love five more times," said she, striking her dainty alabaster fist against his mighty left shoulder, giggling all the while.

It could take me a while to get things properly organized, thought Genghis Twerp. A long time, indeed.

***

CHAPTER NINE

WHEN JOHN TRAWLER REGAINED consciousness, he found himself clutching a small, rectangular object with squiggly things resembling letters and numbers things on it. *A porty-computer?* With trembling eyes, he examined it, and, yeah, it was a porty computer. It seemed to burn his hand with supernal energies. What significance had this multi-tasking thing on an apparently computer hungry planet?

He rose to his slender feet and surveyed the scene. Ahead, the Earth party was lining up their howitzers to slobber-knock down the barriers of Them. Behind, the adequate, reasonably technological (till now, anyway...) on vacation Us army were lining up behind the Earthers, preparing to riddle the ripened Wisconsin (pepper jack) cheese out of Them.

So, that's why the castle was empty! thought John Trawler, his naturally adept well-oiled mind quickly sizing up a situation that others would have pondered for hours, face palming himself in the process. *If I don't warn the crew, their collective and proverbial goose is cooked.*

Suddenly, a thought came to him, with the speed of lightning, roar of thunder. Capped Anthony Spaulding, the ship's private first class (who had unwittingly been caught in the barrage while wandering far too close to the castle for some close-ups of the soon to be marred natural beauty for the crew newsletter and the folks back home), said, "Why should you warn the crew, M'sieur? After all, it was Security Chief Alf Simpson who tried to kill you. Let him stew in this ridiculous situation he's gotten into. As military adviser, it's his responsibility. The Captain will be furious. She'll probably scratch his eyes out and have him castrated. Again."

John Trawler paused a moment in thought. The cold logic was sound except for one niggling detail. "How did you know it was Security Chief Alf Simpson who ordered the barrage?"

"I gave him the idea."

Oh, John Trawler thought, *there's more to this Capped Anthony Spaulding than meets the eye. He has plans. If only I could win him over to my side, we might help bring peace and harmony to the solar system.* He said, "You're right. Let's go into the castle and watch."

At that, the Captain said, "All right, boys, fire! Demolish the whole barricade wall, and don't leave much of it left."

The howitzers fired. Within seconds, the age-old barricade was gone, and the Earthmen found themselves facing the Them army: two hundred thousand peasant shepherds with long pointed sticks.

"Gosh, Captain, do we have to charge?" said Harvey Baines Woofbanger, the ship's new, plucky Lieutenant.

"No more insubordination," the Captain said, almost driven to tears. "Do it—now!"

The first rank of Earthmen charged.

"Bonzai!"

Behind, the Us army, equipped with 4,000 M-1 rifles, were almost ready to shoot.

In the castle, a look of anguished compassion came to John Trawler. "We can't let this happen," he said. "At least three or four of our men are innocent."

"M'sieur," clucked Capped Anthony Spaulding, "we have a saying in my native Marseilles, *C'est Le vie*, which your cruder but still expressive language translates as 'Ehn, easy come, easy go.' They knew the job was dangerous when they signed up, and there are worse ways to die."

"You're right," John Trawler conceded, "but I'm too nice to let it happen anyway." He raised his voice loudly and said, "Men of Earth, look behind you, or meet the doom which I'll confess most of you have earned."

Security Chief Alf Simpson said, "Genghis Twerp *already* fell for that trick. But we sure as heck won't!"

"Heck, no!"

Suddenly, John Trawler realized that despite his lusty voice, no effort of his well-capacitated lungs could carry his logical words the great distance to his doomed companions. Capped Anthony Spaulding realized this also and guffawed. They could do nothing but watch as the first wave of Earthmen, firing their weapons fast and furiously, reached the army of Them. Hand to hand combat raged, and a great cloud of dust rose from the fury and flurry of the fighting. No one could see what was happening amongst the mortal combat, but from the amount of noise and clangor that emanated from the dust cloud, it was obvious the battle was not by any means over. As the second wave of Earthmen moved into position, the army of Us still had not fired.

It came to John Trawler in a flash. Seasoned in battle as the commander of the Us army was, he was waiting for the Captain to commit her reserves. Once she did, she would be helpless. There would be no way for her to counter the new attack, no way for her to shift the weight of her forces. To thwart the whole plan, it was only necessary for one of the crew to look over his shoulder. But John Trawler knew how unlikely this was.

The second wave of Earthmen moved in and soon became completely obscured in the battle already raging. There could be no question, no query of calling them back. Now only a single wave remained. Once this was committed, only a few artillerymen and officers and cooks and barely licensed truck drivers would remain. The Us army could capture the whole works. The crew would be helpless!

John Trawler thought frantically. For him to leave the castle and approach the Earth forces close enough for them to hear him would only result in his death at the hands of the Us forces and would serve no purpose.

His right hand clenched, and he felt painfully the porty-'puter. Supernal and energetic it felt; was it supernal in deed? He raised it high over his head and concentrated, knitting his brow for emphasis.

From somewhere in the Us ranks, there came a mighty congested sneeze. Lieutenant Harvey Baines Woofbanger said, "What was that?" and turned around.

Taking the sneeze as a signal, the Us-men charged! They fired fast and furiously as they attacked. The first volley wiped out the howitzer crews and set a truck on fire. The Captain was winged in the pinky.

"Damn, oh damn, something's always going wrong," she pouted, stamping her little foot. "Security Chief Alf Simpson, do something. You're the ranking military adviser."

"I'm afraid I can't, Captain, my Captain," lied the sly Security Chief Alf Simpson from beneath the chassis of a four-ton truck, "I've been wounded through the left spleen and possibly my heart."

"Oh, no! Oh, no!" The Captain was frantic. She still had a third of her command, but it was facing the wrong way. If only she could think of something to say to them, something direct and witty, but not too harsh or misleading. The Captain cursed her insecurity wrought inner demons; her conversational ineptness came up at the most inopportune times.

The mind of John Trawler, perhaps amplified by the wondrous porty-'puter, perhaps not, reached out to the Earth crew.

It said, piercing their ape-descended minds, *Yo, dudes, you're out-classed, man. Get the Hell off the battlefield.*

The Earthmen, now that blessed retreat had been suggested to their disjointed minds, were more than willing to comply. But it wasn't easy because they were surrounded on two sides by much-determined enemies. The Us troops were riddling them with bullets and butchering them with real pointy bayonets. The men of Them were poking them with their equally jabby pointy sticks and hurting the bejeezus out of them.

"Also remember, the men who are fighting Them can't see what's going on because of a huge dust cloud," Capped Anthony Spaulding said. "Of course, you realize that you've managed to turn a tough but manageable situation into a complete rout. You're well intentioned, John Trawler, but you're also stupid, and not in a good way, either. You should've just told them to turn around."

"Easy come, easy go," replied the witty but virtuous Earthling. "After all, I've never done this before."

And then an idea came to him.

"Now that you've gone this far," said Capped Anthony Spaulding, sarcastically, "why don't you have them surrender?" *Duh.*

Amplified by the porty-phone maybe, John Trawler's mind sent a mental signal to the Captain and to the crew. *Surrender. But don't give yourselves away.*

The nations of Us and Them were known to have long maintained peace in their part of Part of Upper Uranus. Admittedly, they had used the rather unorthodox method of conventional friendly hostility. What counted was that their hearts were in the right place, no wonder which side they beat on. Perhaps they would keep ten or twelve Earthlings as slaves, and John Trawler could save them; whereas, if the battle continued, there was little hope.

"Surrender. Yeah, good idea," the Captain said, "glad I

thought of it." She twirled her hair for emphasis. "Hey, boys, surrender now. Let's talk sense into those Uranians. I'm sure we can win them over to our pacifist ways."

The fighting continued. The Captain took her garter belt off, crawled under a tractor, and waved it in the air to signify and emphasize her desire for parley.

Immediately, the peace-loving armies of Us and Them stopped firing and made for the Captain to negotiate. The 3,927 ambulatory Earthmen left on the field were handcuffed but otherwise left unharmed. The Captain was not so lucky; forced to jog multiple laps around the tractor to keep ahead of the people of Us-Them, who proved to be eager negotiators. The ship's band struck up the traditional classic *Benny Hill Theme*.

John Trawler watched the long column of prisoners limping towards Them. He turned to Capped Anthony Spaulding. "As Earthmen, it is our sworn and sacred God-given duty to rescue them."

Capped Anthony Spaulding arched an eyebrow for emphasis. "You're kidding, right?"

"Besides, if we don't, we'll never be able to return to Earth," countered John Trawler, logically. "Uranus will remember us only as an unhappy episode from the distant past. We will never be able to convince them of our naturally harmonious natures, balanced by Yin and Yang. I shudder to think what will happen if they ever attain to space travel."

Capped Anthony Spaulding thought, *No more lobster dinners. I'll be stuck here forever living on Uranian snails. Blech!* Though Capped Anthony Spaulding was not naturally a humanitarian, grossly imagined or otherwise, not even he on a cold summer morning after the blessed dew could resist John Trawler's powerful, yet logical oration.

They marched to the dented battlements of the castle and shouted in union, "Men of Earth, we will lead you! Come to the castle and be safe!"

In a surprisingly short space of time, 1.500 Earth crewmen, drunk during the battle and thus not there, showed up at the castle gate.

By nightfall, another two thousand who had been playing dead on the battleground showed up. A surprised John Trawler coldly calculated that only three or four actual Earth men died in the furiously contested conflagration which had lasted two days.

SOMEWHERE IN THE KRANCKY Mountains, a child was rescued from his water-logged basket, and as the child was learning to walk, thinking of his mother who was dying while his father stared beatifically at the setting sun which shone through her cell at the Asylum for Virgin Mothers, and neither of them knew where their son was being raised or whether he was alive.

It was raining.

***

CHAPTER TEN

THE TELEPHONE RANG. *I wish I had had an elevator installed when I had the chance,* thought the Big King Twerp as he climbed the steps to Telephone Tower. After a seemingly interminable climb, regularly penetrated by the high-pitched scream of the telephone siren, Big King Twerp, at last, answered the phone.

"Hear you've got quite a crowd over there, King Twerp, fella. How goes it?"

"Great, just great, you misbegotten product of the union of a carp and a telephone repairman. Your long-distance phone calling days are almost over. I'm going to have you strangled in a dark mountain pass."

The mysterious voice paused and then said, lowering their pear shaped dulcet tones for more emphasis, "Things are pretty lousy, right?"

"No, they're great! They're great, I tell ya! I'm going to have you murdered, you sad sack of salami! Don't you understand? You aren't going to be able to torment me any longer!"

"You have a short temper for a happy man."

"Take a walk."

"Show me a sample of your handwriting. In cursive, please."

Big King Twerp hung up. One could only take oh so much, and he had been under a great strain ever since Ish had returned with his horde of Thugs. They weren't exactly the well-disciplined source of massive destruction he had thought them to be. Plus they stank. Horribly. If he didn't get his march of conquest under way soon, Antwerp would be a leveled wasteland, teenage or otherwise.

Ish met him on the stairway. "Don't go into the throne room, Your Mass Entropy, the Thugs, are carting off the gold ornaments. I'd hate to see what happened if you disturbed them.

"I'll kill them!"

"Temper, temper, Your Mass Entropy. We don't want to destroy our invasion force. At least not yet."

"I'll kill them."

"Think of it as an investment in your future."

"I'll kill them."

"See if you can arrange for it to happen on the battlefield."

"No, I can't wait. We must kill them now while Antwerp still stands. I'll murdelize da bums."

"It's a little late for that, Your Mass Entropy. Through all Antwerp, not a gold statue or copper spoon remains unmelted or unsmelted"

A resounding thud bopped on the door to the castle stairs. Crude Thuggish voices garbled out, "Perhaps this door leads to more gold."

"After you, Gaston."

"No, no, after you, Alphonse." And so it went, on and on and on and on.

Ish said, "Look, Your Mass Entropy, all we have to do is hold on until the Earthmen get here. Then we can use their Captain, oh their Captain, to build a mighty disciplined fighting force."

"This was my master plan," said Big King Twerp of Antwerp as regally as he could for added emphasis, "but the Earthmen have been beaten and perhaps permanently stalled. In other words, they've forked up. Unless...." And a piercing,

51

malevolent look of dead grandeurs came to his eyes— "Unless John Trawler is in possession of the ONE TRUE PORTY-'PUTER. Then he may be able to lead them to safety, and to our very gates."

Downstairs, outside the door, there came a loud, thunderous belch. The door shattered into thousands of small iron splinters which ricocheted throughout the staircase, pinging and zinging all about.

"They're coming. Quick, to the Tower! We can bolt the adamantium door. Hurry, Your Mass Entropy, hurry."

And so the legendary Siege of Telephone Tower began.

"That's funny," said Botter, a surreptitious, intermediate-sized Thug with a tassel cap he had claimed from Big King Twerp's closet and was proud of, pushing past the still preppondering Gaston and Alphonse. "I don't see no gold."

"Yeah," said another, Notter, his brother, not nearly an exact fraternal twin, but still bearing an acute semblance all the same,"look at all those flights of stairs! There must be lots and lots of it at the top."

Three hundred Thugs, acting as three hundred, charged up the first two or three flights of stairs.

"One good thing," said Ish, as Big King Twerp and he huddled in the Tower chamber; "the Thugs'll probably never make it up all sixteen flights of stairs. They've gotten out of shape during their soft stay at the palace. If one of them in front topples, he'll carry the whole bunch back down. Ka-thud."

"I like that," said Big King Twerp of Antwerp.

The telephone rang.

Big King Twerp and Ish looked at each other uneasily. Could it, perhaps, be a wrong number? Someone announcing that Big King Twerp of Antwerp had won the "Corky Sow is cute in 25 words or less" contest? An invitation to eat Thanksgiving dinner with the relatives, distant or otherwise?

Ish picked up the phone.

"Sorry, but Big King Twerp isn't in just now. Can I take a message?"

"Tell him I want him, I need him; I must have him!" cried a strangely high-pitched voice. There was a sudden click, then the dial tone.

"I want you, I need you, I must have you."

"Ish?!" cried the astonished King, backing towards the doorway.

"Not me, Your Mass Entropy, him."

"Who?" gibbered Big King Twerp, his bulging eyes searching wildly throughout the tiny tower room.

"The man on the phone."

"The man on the phone?"

"Yes, that's right, the man on the phone."

"You say, it's the man on the phone?"

"Correct."

"There's no man on the phone! The room's empty, you lying scum. You're trying to drive me bats. Bats, I say! Bats! Bats! Bats! It won't work! It won't work! It won't work! It won't work!"

So saying, Big King Twerp grabbed an ornamental spear hanging from above the tower fireplace. Ish threw the telephone at him, with bullseye accuracy. Luckily, they had just installed an extra long cord as Big King Twerp was wont to wander about while dreaming up clever replies to his frequent caller, and Ish's aim being true, it struck him square on the nape of the neck as if applied as unto a certain nerve pinch.

Big King Twerp of Antwerp slid to the floor, drooling and unconscious.

As Ish breathed a ragged sigh of relief, a softly imploring voice drifted through the small tower window.

"Help me! Help me!" said an incandescently beautiful tiny female flying creature, obviously from the Realms of Faerie. "I come from the fairy micro-kingdom of Tsallio. We are menaced by

53

the Great Pale Death from beyond the stars."

"Really?"

"Yes. An oracle said, 'Go to Big King Twerp of Aut*werp*.

He is wise.

He can help you.'"

"Wrong kingdom. This is *Ant*werp," said Ish, winging her with a snub-nosed .38. He returned his attention to the door, through which he heard the sound of approaching thudding Thuggish footsteps.

"Boy, I'm winded!" said a voice. "The gold up here better be good, and if it isn't, let's kill and maim and plunder the living heck out of it all anyway."

"Duh, okay."

Ish grabbed the ornamental spear from Big King Twerp's limp hands. He rushed to the iron door. Knowing that this door, like the one to the staircase, would never be able to withstand the litany of Thugs' foul belches, and also keeping in mind that it would be easier to kill a winded, gasping, wheezing Thug than a rested one, he flung open the huge iron contrivance and rushed the startled but bloodthirsty though tired poorly postured humanoids without. The first one fell immediately. So did the second. The third turned to flee but only succeeded in causing even more cacophonous confusion. Ish had no compunctions about stabbing him in the back and pushing him willy-nilly into the staircase. The Thugs proceeded to fall all over each other (being so winded from the climb that they were hardly able to stand in the first place). Ish moved among them, killing and maiming, sticking and stabbing. He heard the cry from below, "The Tower hides the demon Tele-Phone, woe to us for we have released his dire and unrelenting wrath."

A great wailing followed, shouts for mercy, and, "For the love of Pegleg Pete, get out of my way, you fool!"

Soon the siege was ended. But the phone rang again. Big

King Twerp woke up, saying, "Ish, we need something to distract us from the damned ringing. Bring forth the ALL-SEEING EYE of Antwerp, which we cleverly moved up here these three days hence to protect from roaming Thugs."

Ish brought the EYE out. "No good. All I'm picking up are weather reports and a rerun of a live soap opera. Wait—no—here comes the wonderful Wizard!"

They listened to the latest on the progression of the Earth-expedition, interspersed with a panel discussion of the possible whereabouts of Genghis Twerp.

Downstairs, five hundred gold-crazed Thugs, unconvinced as is ever their wont by the panicked stories of the two hundred ninety Thugs who had just returned, panting and sweating, from the Tower, prepared to mount an attack up the sixteen flights of stairs.

The phone continued ringing.

***

CHAPTER ELEVEN

FOR A DAY, THE Earthmen rested. They needed to think up a suitable strategy and let the potential rescuees stew for a while in juices of their making.

"The first thing we need to do is re-capture 'the howitzers,'" John Trawler was explaining, trying very hard not to use his hands for added emphasis.

"Right, righeet!" agreed the strangely agreeable Capped Anthony Spaulding, reeling about through various richly-ornamented though badly smoke-damaged compartments of the castle, his picture taking device strangely still unscathed from the awesome onslaught.

"But, even before we do that, we have to find some way to pry the men from the wine cellars that lie beneath our feet," continued John Trawler.

"Whyee don we brin de wieen up heer?" suggested the grinning private first class.

John Trawler was confused. Perhaps Capped Anthony Spaulding was not thinking along the same lines as him. He thought about wielding the porty-'puter once again. Would it work this time? At any rate, it would probably not worsen their situation.

He pulled the 'puter out of his wallet and concentrated: *Men, take the howitzers.* A handful of men, looking peculiarly ruddy-ish about the cheeks and eyes, came straggling up to ground level. Brad McKray and Joel McKray, who looked more stolid-minded than most, wandered as one over to John Trawler. "Did the Captain say something about taking the howitzers?"

"She did indeed. Round up the men, go forth, and make a brave charge of it, and there'll be steaks for you all. There are steers and beer aplenty in the Them stockades."

"Oh, yeah?" said McKray. "I didn't know that."

Brad McKray said, "Sure, Joel, why would there be all these pesky sharp jabby stick herdsmen if they didn't have steers? Steer-herders. Get it? Ha, har, ha!" Joel McKray got a puzzled frown and slapped Brad McKray in the cheek. Brad McKray tweaked Joel McKray's nose. They fell together and rolled in the dust, cuffing, poking, guffawing, and biting.

"Say there, Sarge, y'know it ain gonna work," said the private first class. "Dose men ain't gonna do nothin' for days. An' they sure ain't gonna rush no howitzers. They do that, and they'll be des-stroyed!!" Capped Anthony Spaulding evilly chuckled an evil chuckle.

"You might have a point there," nodded John Trawler with concern. "But there's no hope for bettering our lives if we don't try to free the others. Think of it—a life full of snail—"

John Trawler and Capped Anthony Spaulding (and Brad McKray and Joel McKray, ceasing their brawl to follow the interesting older duo) walked down the gravel-crusted stairs to the underground pit where the wine was, and the men were. These men were reclined on divans, lolled over couches, and otherwise enjoying the sumptuous furnishings of what remained of the underground of the badly wrecked (and charred) castle. Many of them appeared badly influenced by the large, vast quantities of wine which ran from the gorged red corners of their mouths. Tasty stuff, that.

"These men are drunk!" shouted Capped Anthony Spaulding, displaying an unexpected burst of moral indignation.

"Is this military discipline? Have you any respect for your Captain, who now lies languishing in some sordid Them prison? Come; make a charge of it; we can take Them and Us by surprise!"

John Trawler was greatly impressed to hear Capped Anthony Spaulding talk so responsibly, albeit to no discernible effect. The men paid them no heed. He concentrated thickly again, clutching the hand-'puter until it nicked his hand. *Come men! To arms! For the Captain! For Earth! For freeeedom! For good, fresh steak!*

Two more men rose slowly to their feet. "Steak, huh?"

"Good, *fresh* steak...."

"Non-vegan?"

"But, of course!"

"Ooooo...."

Emboldened by his telepathic success, John Trawler said, "There are six of us standing, so we can't make a frontal charge of it. Let us sneak out to the battlefield, assess the situation militarily, and see how we can best effect our army's rescue."

"Effect or affect?" asked Capped Anthony Spaulding.

"What?"

"Never mind...."

Walking two abreast, they soon reached the unguarded battlefield (Good! The Us-Them armies, flushed with their victory, had underestimated—though not by much—the possibility of the Earth survivors making a comeback against all odds, much like the semi-mythical Tim Tebow lo those many years ago!)

John Trawler's face shone with the flush of an able man exercising his potential for leadership. "We're going to make a three-pronged attack of it, men. Brad McKray and Joel McKray will crawl through the window of that limestone building where, I sense, the bulk of our army is held prisoner. Take advantage of their large numbers to un-handcuff them, one by one, inconspicuously. Then tell them to high-tail it for the castle, lickety-split. Many will be picked off, but if you stay in the middle of our army, you'll stand a good chance of making it back alive and possibly even in one piece.

"Richard and Scammon *(the other two. We hadn't named them yet, but John Trawler thought up names.—Da Authors)* will make a bee-line for that blue-green pillbox."

"Why?"

"The Captain and other first officers are being interrogated there." John Trawler hoped that his shrewd, coldly calculated through sheer logic guesses would prove right. (After all, many trusted his guesses more than others' facts!) But his voice betrayed no lack of confidence, not even a warbling smidgen. "Stun all the guards with your hand phasers and hasten our officers quietly back to the castle. In the greater commotion from the limestone building, you probably won't be noticed.

Capped Anthony Spaulding and I will remain here by the howitzers. If a large contingent of soldiers comes running after our men, we'll hold them off until they retreat, or our troops get to safety, or we get killed, which is a distinct possibility, I'm afraid."

"You're afraid?" asked Scammon.

"What?"

"You said you were...never mind," finished Dick.

Fortunately, Capped Anthony Spaulding, totally absorbed in a boxy electronic object that could store the contents of up to five penny dreadfuls, hadn't heard the last part of the plan.

"Hop to it, men!"

Scammon and Dick ran enthusiastically for the pillbox in a calculated serpentine motion, zagging and zigging, and then zagging again, a pillbox whose gun swiveled gradually in their direction, almost lackadaisically. Then it fired a series of eighteen rapid-fire shots, which systematically pounded the two men to atoms despite their rather competent fancy footwork.

Capped Anthony Spaulding looked up from his thriller.

"Say, Holmes, that part of the plan didn't work too good!"

John Trawler peered anxiously after Brad McKray and Joel McKray, who were making a more cautious way toward the large limestone building.

"Say there, uh, Joel McKray, do ya think all those guards on the roof'll be pickin' us off?"

"Guards? Roof?" asked Joel McKray, eating ground in his frantic panic.

"Just pulling your leg," said Brad McKray with a wry grin. "Sucker."

Joel McKray, who was short, fat, bow-legged, and good-natured—Brad McKray was skinny, tall, crew-cut, and saturnine—said, "Geez, Brad McKray, you shouldn't do that, knowing how high strung I am."

"Actually, I think it's pretty strange they don't have any guards posted if they're keeping 4,000 or so odd prisoners in here."

"I see what you mean. Hey, I just had a thought. What if the ground next to the building, upon which we are about to set foot, is..."

The resulting explosion was near deafening.

"Mined! Blast it, Capped Anthony Spaulding, now only you and I remain to save our forces."

"Ya mean only *you* are left, cuz. I'm goin' back to the castle."

"No, you can't! Capped old fellow, the whole plan hinges on your cool eye, steady nerves, and sure judgment."

"'I'm sure gonna put Judgment off a few years more. I'll go and drink some Budweiser American Ale. Gnoamsayen?" Capped Anthony Spaulding sauntered happily away from the scene of battle.

John Trawler, his mind hazed with desperation, pointed the porty-'puter at Capped Anthony Spaulding and thought, *Come and do my bidding. We must create a diversion with the howitzers while our men escape.'* Capped Anthony Spaulding kept shambling away, apparently unaffected.

Suddenly, the private first class jumped in the air, kicked his heels, cried, "Yahoo!" and sped precipitously back to the howitzers. With a blow from the unexpectedly powerful back of his left hand, he brushed John Trawler off his feet, jumped to the nearest Big Gun and started firing.

"Yes. Yes. Blow up the enemy. Wipe 'em all out!"

"Capped Anthony Spaulding! You're firing at the building that has our army in it!"

"No, there ain't gonna be no war no mo', there ain't gonna be no war—"

Blam. Bat. Bam. Bang.

A white flag rose through a gaping hole in the limestone building.

"Capped Anthony Spaulding, our men are trying to surrender."

The private first class let off one last salvo. Then his face froze in a demented grin, and he fell over backward.

John Trawler wondered what internal effects his use of the porty-'puter was having on people.

For a split second, the private first class seemed to metamorphose—into a mushroom? No. No. Then he was his usual grinning self again, albeit frozen motionless on the ground.

Then, to John Trawler's delighted consternation, the entire imprisoned Earth army, led by the Captain, the first officer, and Security Chief Alf Simpson, trooped out; not from the big building but from the pillbox!

In a flurry of excitement, Joel McKray and Brad McKray of the Earth McKrays, who were not dead but were still alive, explained what had transpired to John Trawler. After the mine blast had barely missed them, they had decided to head for the less-imposing-looking pillbox, which for some reason had not fired at them.

"Ah!" John Trawler said. "The delicate robot mechanism inside the pillbox must have been temporarily disabled by the mine blast tremor."

There was a robot mechanism inside but no Us-Them guards. A passageway led underneath the pillbox to an underground chamber where the Earth army was chained up. Joel McKray and Brad McKray of the Earth McKrays had freed them.

But who was in the limestone building? The Earth forces never took the time to find out, but it was the armies of Them and Us who had been temporarily stunned by the caving in of their roof by howitzer fire, but they were soon awake again and hungry for Earth blood.

For their courage and heroism, Joel McKray and Brad McKray of the Earth McKrays were both made corporals. John Trawler, to the disdain of Security Chief Alf Simpson and the more dismay of Lieutenant Harvey Baines Woofbanger, was made the new Ensign, ranking par with Harvey Baines Woofbanger, who hadn't been much help in the battle and had nearly lost his man card over it, to boot.

The Earth forces, minus the six men who had given up their lives on the hideous battlefield, regrouped and, after making a wide detour around Them, began again to head along Route 66 towards More of Them by the Sea.

And, for the time being, here their story ends.

***

CHAPTER TWELVE

THE ALL-SEEING EYE blared loudly, drowning out the repeated peal of the telephone and the thousand angry feet pounding up the stairs.

"What do you think, Babahwahba? Have we seen anything like it before?"

"I don't know, Jim Lewah. These Earthmen are really pretty dumb; you know? They had all the odds in their favor for conquering this part of the world, but they keep throwing their opportunities away. If they weren't such damn cowards, they'd already be all dead."

"Come on, Babahwaba; you gotta give 'em a little more credit than that. I think this Lieutenant Harvey Baines Woofbanger at least has some real leadership qualities going for him. How do you see it, Walter?"

"I never analyze. I'm moderator and father figure. Coldbeer, how do you sum it up?"

"Whatever the Earthmen do is merely a pawn's game. We're going to see the main action in this, THE BEGINNING OF THE GREAT WAR FOR TOTAL DOMINION OF PART OF UPPER URANUS coming from two sources: The Big King Twerp in his palace at Antwerp, and Genghis Twerp, present whereabouts unknown. Sooner or later they'll mobilize all of the various races, kingdoms, and villages into a real big two-way war, in which all of the land will be laid waste. This is, you know, basically a blood feud between the House of Twerp, since Genghis Twerp and The Big are half-brothers, though neither of them yet know it. *Frere de mon frere.*"

"It isn't true! It isn't. It isn't. Ahhhhhhhh!!!" cried the Big King Twerp, almost like a big baby, striking the ALL-SEEING EYE with his hammy fist and standing solidly in a blind stupor.

"Come on, Chief, I'm listening," said Ish as he plugged it back in.

"Thank you, Coldbeer. Fairan Balanced?"

"I think you're exaggerating the importance of Genghis Twerp. Yea and truly. He may already be dead, for all we know."

"I hope so," sighed Big King Twerp. "I never did like him, you know. He would always pee upstream of me whenever we'd go swimming. Bastard."

"We know. And all his previous track record shows is that he's good at organizing small bands of cut-throats, leading them into the thick of battle, and then getting them wiped out by more technologically superior advanced forces. Remember in '67, when he led all those man-toads off a cliff?"

"Thanks, Fairan Balanced. Here comes what we've all been waiting for, folks. A live, in-depth report on D'Wharf civilization just before it gets obliterated, from Tom and Dick."

"Hi, guys. We don't have much to say, really. These folks drink a lot; they smoke a lot. But they *are* noble and polite."

"Here you see a picture of their village. They really do have about the most highly advanced culture around. See all the libraries? And art museums! Boy, do they have art museums."

"Do you think the D'Wharfs will accept death complacently, as they have accepted life?"

"Yeah, probably. And nobly and politely, even."

"By the way, guys, do you know how far the Earthmen are from town? Good news coverage is one thing, but staying around to get killed is quite yet another."

"You might as well take off now, boys. If you want, you can circle back to town after the battle and report on the remains."

Meanwhile, some two dozen of the Thugs, taking a wrong turn on the stairs, had run right out of the Tower at the tenth flight and plummeted to a sure and smucky, vertigo-inducing death. The survivors, fearing a terrifying intervention by some supernatural agency, retreated to the palace proper.

Big King Twerp interrupted, his voice tinged with mounting annoyance. "So, what I get from you men is that the central question we're trying to deal with is 'Is it the ONE PORTY-PHONE or isn't it?'"

The commentators stared at the camera. "We never said that."

"Nope. Never, never, ever."

"To answer this vital question, we must go to the original owner of the ONE TRUE PORTY-'PUTER, the Wizard himself." Walter gulped audibly. "Wizard, you're on the air."

***

CHAPTER THIRTEEN

BRAD MCKRAY AND JOEL McKray, marching rigidly in formation, skipped merrily along Route 66. "Hey, what do you think of the latest issue?" Brad McKray was reading from *The Earth-Uranus Monthly*, the unofficial crew news organ. It told about the rout of Us. *We marched peacefully to their mean, heavily fortified city, waving olive branches. But they fired at us. So we killed them all. Afterward, I interviewed one of them, a dying cop. He said, 'Ya know, you guys treated us fair and square. We deserved to die, shootin' at you and all. Wev learned are lessins.' Then this guy dyed.*

"Hey, is that how the battle really went?" Joel McKray asked, scratching his philtrum with reckless abandon.

Brad McKray shrugged, mugging extra hard for emphasis. "I *don't* remember back that far."

Joel McKray shrugged as well, but with far less mugging, emphasizing nothing. "Me neither."

Lieutenant Harvey Baines Woofbanger walked beside them in abject, total shock. He had been born in Providence, Rhode Island, and brought up expecting to do good things despite his never ending fear of all things cosmic horror. After he had graduated from high school and the military academy, he was immediately wafted onto the Uranus expedition. Shortly after landing on the planet, they had made him an Ensign (he had kept saving the ship time and time again, even under the absurdest of means on a nearly weekly syndicated basis.) Now it had been taken away from him, and he was a nobody again. He stared ahead in soul-shattering disbelief.

"Come on, Harv," said Joel McKray, a kind-hearted soul, big on heart, but, alas, equally lacking in brains and common sense. "It ain't so bad. Your mother didn't die or nothing."

"Who cares about Mom?"

"Aha! See!"

"My promotion. My promotion," he whispered, more to himself than to anyone else. Saliva ran softly from the corners of his mouth, his hair grew unkempt, and his eyes widened.

John Trawler was exceedingly happy. Now that he was Ensign, he would have—was having—significant input in crew decisions. When they got to More of Them by the Sea, it would be to exchange gifts and share important, friendship-building secrets that would lead to true peace and understanding on both Earth and Uranus.

CAPTAIN'S LOG, APRIL 19 (Written by Security Chief Alf Simpson): So hear we are walkin along getin redy to hit another city I dont like this John Trawler's attitude at all. This is off the record, but I think the Captain likes him because he goes for the guys with skinny legs. The Captain, I mean. But Im worrid about him tryin to turn this expaddition into some kinda peacenik orgey. Anyway, we reached the village without further inceedent.

We started hauling up the big guns again and John Trawler, he says what did we want to do that for hed hav are men arrested for insupportanation. I said no he coldnt because I was still his superior oficer and he said no an ensigns hier in rank. I said heck with that noise lets ask the Captain but I didnt relly want to ask him because then he might agree with John Trawler and we woodnt have a batle on are hands.

CAPPED ANTHONY SPAULDING SAID, "Why don' you pull the old white flag trick again?"

Security Chief Alf Simpson said, "Huh?"

"Have the Captain send John Trawler into More-of-Them-by-the-Sea to parley for peace. Then shell the living hell out of the city."

The plan worked like a charm. Soon John Trawler, leading a deputation of twenty hair-crested soldiers, marched lovingly into the city. Ten minutes later, the Captain, confused with unhappiness, said, "Where is he, where is he? He's been gone for ten minutes; do you think he's in trouble?"

"Sorry to say, Cap'n, but he *daid*. Our men report he got shot as he entered the city."

"Oh! How mean of them. How very mean!'" She pouted and stamped her little foot. "Mr. Security Chief Alf Simpson, shell the city until it rots. Take no prisoners."

"Glad to oblige, Captain. Men, haul up the Big Barts!"

"Wooo!"

With a rousing cheer, the Earth peoples hauled their little, medium, and massive weapons into place and began shooting.

John Trawler wore a bright, many-colored uniform, as did his men, who also played on brass instruments a resounding chorus of "Give peace a chance."

High King Celibate looked out of his royal bedroom window and thought, *What the Bloody ding dong hell is that? I haven't authorized any marching bands. Wake me out of my royal sleep will they? I'll have them by the palm trees!*

Kissing his soundly sleeping wife on the forehead, the High King Celibate slipped on his lemon green bathrobe and clapped for his six royal guards. With them marching behind, he strolled onto the veranda and yelled, "What the ruddy fornication are you men doing out on the street?"

John Trawler gave his most winning smile and bowed

almost to the pavement. A chill wind blew the last gray leaf of Autumn along the street. "Your imperial majesty, we come from Earth bringing gay tidings of Peace and Friendliness to the enlightened territory of More of Them by the Sea."

"Oh, well, I suppose we'll have to have them in to tea. Siv," he said, pitching his voice to the basement quarters where the burly Gnorwegian lived, "see to the buttered scones and crumpets, will you?"

One of the Earth party, hungry for good real food, said, "Do you have any seed cake? I like seed cake."

"As do I!" chimed in another.

"Lots!" the High King Celibate found himself saying before he caught himself.

"And steaming ale! And prunes!" said other Earthers, rousing themselves with gastronomical excitement.

"My goodness," mumbled Siv, who overheard all this, to himself, "these men ban seem to know High King Celibate's larder as well as I do."

"Well," the High King Celibate whispered to him from across the hall, "if the rations run short, you know their duty as good guests. They'll have to do without."

Soon the Earth parley and High King Celibate and his Queen and several of the High King' Celibate's eating-drinking buddies were sitting around a large rectangular table full of dark turkey, eating it.

"Ya, sure, I cook good don't I, your highness," said Siv.

"Siv," said the High King Celibate, waxing his whole noble and polite mouth ecstatic over an especially well-done grape, "you're boss, you know that? Real boss. Styling, even."

"I tink that sure was one compliment. Yes, sure. You ban like more coffee?"

"I've got a good story," said Jedediah Starm, a short, squat, ugly, albeit highly smart but drug-freaked Earthman. "Gertrude

69

and Heathcliffe. Gertrude and Heathcliffe. There are these two seagulls walking along this bridge, see, and one of them says, 'Thou knowest that there's only room for one seagull on this bridge. So the other one pushes him off. Ha!" There was noble and polite applause from the D'wharfs at the table, save the High King Celibate, from whom it was considered not proper to applaud anything, but John Trawler and the Earth Folk, who had heard the story before, ignored it, as was their custom.

Paragon, whose still excitable character was moved to excitement by this exciting situation, jumped up on the table and started walking on turkey meat, singing "Give my regards to Au— Twerp."

"I say," said the High King Celibate, who was a very proper noble and polite gentleman and insisted on impeccable good manners, "Bad form! Bad form!"

The ale flowed freely.

A tall, respectable gentleman in a tuxedo and clothes came to the table and whispered in the High King Celibate's ear. "The Hot-Line, sir. It's Gilfgilf."

"Gilfgilf!" High King Celibate started to roar aloud, then catching himself, "He's always good for a few laughs. Heh. Heh. Yes, I'll talk to him."

The High King Celibate said he had to powder his nose, then opened the secret trap door in the dining room ceiling which led to his secret Hot-Line, and, boosted on Siv's humongous shoulders, climbed to it, and sealed the door unnoticed and unobtrusively behind him. He picked up the receiver.

"Hi, Gilf. Say, you don't mind if I call you Gilf for short, do you?"

"High King Celibate, you're in one hell of a lot of trouble. I realize the palace is soundproofed, so you may not know yet that the town has been getting drilled for half an hour. The Earth army is doing it; there are even more of them than I thought there'd be.

There's absolutely no hope of even one D'wharf surviving. So, I'm leaving town right now, this very instant. Bye."

The High King Celibate gave little credence to Gilfgilf's words, but nonetheless returned to the dinner table concerned and sullen, yet still noble and polite.

"SAY THERE, BRAD MCKRAY; you know Capped Anthony Spaulding?"

"Who doesn't?" replied Brad Mckray.

"Well, wasn't that him who just turned into a giant mushroom on the road right in front of us?"

"Come on, old man Joel McKray. Ya know it's me who pulls the sight gags, not you." But, as Brad McKray looked ahead, he saw—a giant mushroom!—and as he looked, it metamorphosed back to Capped Anthony Spaulding.

The Captain, highly enthused by the situation (a whole town full of pacifists, ripe for plunder!) swallowed half a dozen executive red dex and yelled, "Go, Go, Get em, Boys. Yahoo! Google!"

Security Chief Alf Simpson growled in a deep sonorous voice, maintaining his personal mantra, "Kill. Kill. Kill. Kill."

Lieutenant Harvey Baines Woofbanger hid behind a dozen tough-looking fighters and drooled.

Everywhere there was carnage. Everywhere there was slaughter. Everywhere there was surprised looks on dead D'wharfs murdered in their beds or in their siestas.

It was not yet noon.

And it was not raining.

A thousand Earth maimers broke into an expensive dinner theater and picked off 38 young male and female D'wharfs in the middle of watching a new musical comedy before the final curtain. Elsewhere, a fireman's 40th-anniversary party got interrupted and promptly obliterated. (*We wish you could see the whole scene for yourself, dear reader. It was picturesque.—Da Editors)*

IT OCCURRED TO THE Captain to ask Security Chief Alf Simpson, who was reloading his three shotguns, "Security Chief Alf Simpson, if John Trawler and his deputation were killed by the people of this town, why aren't they lying out to bleed somewhere?"

"Incineration, Captain. Incineration," Capped Anthony Spaulding said. "It's their way."

"Oh."

"SAY, YOUR MAJESTY. I sure did call the corner grocery to see if they ban had your favorite elderberry wine. But their phone she was off the hook."

High King Celibate grew even more concerned but as yet said nothing.

THE WHOLE TOWN OF More of Them by the Sea was not very wide, so after a few mere hours: *Captain's Log, April 21ˢᵗ (written by Capped Anthony Spaulding): we had through hard, valorous fighting, beaten a path to shining sea itself. Sea Ontheskale! Never have I seen such a beautiful piece of liquid! Unfortunately, it was liquid helium, as we discovered when one of the men tried to drink from it. He's no good to us now.*

"Summa youse men comb back and wipe out all the survivors," said Security Chief Alf Simpson, who was thoroughly in control of the whole situation. "And remember, their expectin' ya this time.'

Most of us, a motley enough group; reclined on the sides of the Sea and rested. We'd had enough fighting for the day. Brad McKray and Joel McKray, who are often good for a moment's amusement, were making poking feints at one another's eyes while rapping each other's heads.

I rested my toes and spread 'em out in the air. The clouds above filled my soul with peace.

JOHN TRAWLER ROSE FROM the table, happy and bloated. "Begging your pardon, Your Highness, but I must adjourn briefly to confer with my superiors and tell them about our new found links to cooperation and peace." He smiled, did a brief tap-dance, and walked out of the palace.

SECURITY CHIEF ALF SIMPSON SAID, "There's the son of a bitch! Shoot him before the Captain shows up!"

John Trawler was upset by what he saw: a large, bloodstained force of surly Earthers and a nearly non-existent population of quivering D'wharfs.

"Security Chief Alf Simpson, is this another one of your crude and ill-timed jokes?" We must pardon John Trawler, the only thoughtful, intelligent Earthling in this story so far, for making such a dumb comment. He was pretty drunk at the time.

Security Chief Alf Simpson frowned and yelled, "Kill! Kill 'em, men! Shoot 'em in the head! Bang! Bang! Kill!" John Trawler guessed that Security Chief Alf Simpson, overwrought by his apparently successful devastation of the whole town entire, had taken leave of his normal addled senses. He beat a hasty retreated into the palace, bolting the adamantium steel door behind him.

HE WALKED SHYLY BACK into the dining room. He shook his head, sighing to himself. Too bad he had to break up the fun.

"High King Celibate and everybody, I think you ought to know that while we nobly and politely celebrated in here, the rest of the Earth forces, less respectful than we, made a violent end of More of Them by the Sea and its entire population. Now they're laying siege to the palace."

The High King Celibate said, nobly and politely, "I know. I

know. But, hey, what am I supposed to do about it?"

Paragon smiled to himself satisfied, patting himself for extra emphasis. "Now I know what those two guys were talking about."

ELSEWHERE ...

"All right, you got the TNT lined up all around the palace?"

"Sure thing, Chief Military Officer Security Chief Alf Simpson."

The Captain, carried in a bomb-proof canvas divan by 38 loyal adjutants, said, "How's it going, Alf? The palace putting up much resistance?"

"None. In ten seconds, it'll get blown up. Ka-blooey!"

The Captain petitely smiled. "John Trawler will be avenged." She thought about ripping her shirt, as was space trekking Earth captain custom, but thought different of it.

BADBADBABBABBABOOM!!

The palace blew up in a hideous explosion, completely and utterly destroyed.

The Captain shed a lone tear that trickled down her face and into her handsome bosom.

Is John Trawler dead?

***

CHAPTER FOURTEEN

GILFGILF HAD WOKEN THAT morning and immediately, as had been his practice for several days, looked through his binoculars fastened around his neck, at the surrounding plain. He saw the Earth armies off in the distance on Route 66. But it should take them about two hours to get to town. Time for him to try to put his plan into action.

Gilfgilf ran out on the street shrieking hysterically, "The Bip Citters are coming! The Bip Citters are coming! Prepare to evacuate!"

Those few D'wharfs who were up at 9 AM smiled at him placidly and sipped orange-aid.

Gilfgilf put up signs throughout the span of the city reading, "Important town meeting. Come to Central Park immediately. Free popcorn." A few dozen people strolled casually into the park and asked, "Where's the popcorn?"

"I lied to you. There isn't any popcorn." The crowd started to disperse immediately. "But if you stay in town for another 98 minutes, you'll get something even better—free death!!"

"Ahh, what's he talking about?"

"The Bip-Citty Peril will hit More of Them by the Sea almost immediately. No prisoners or anything, but total devastation. If you don't want it that way, get on your wagons and vamoose from town; like right now. Forget your kitties."

"Who is this crank?" asked a bespectacled little old lady without any shoes holding onto a dead cat that she had just previously ironed.

"I dunno," shrugged an obesely overweight yoga instructor with a fish on a leash.

The crowd dispersed. Several of them, hungry for popcorn, went to the movies to watch *Flying Saucers—Gone Tomorrow*.

Gilfgilf tried all of his plans—there were seven of them, all in descending order, none of which succeeded in concerning any of the D'Wharf populace. Finally, in sheer desperation, he took to sky-writing: "Bip Citty is after you. Look out your windows and run."

The pleasant D'Wharf folk looked up and said, "What are they advertising now?"

"Cactus Cola?" guessed one very perplexed citizen.

"A baby's arm holding an apple?" replied another, blinking.

"Beats the black and blue heck out of me," said one local municipal official nobly and politely, "but at least the spelling is correct for a change."

Eventually, the Bip-City folk arrived at the city's gates as one ginormous gibbering horde.

Sadly, soon blood, death, and gore became the norm, like earth, wind, and fire.

Gilfgilf went from building to as yet unshelled building advising folk to either fight back or beat a hasty retreat. They cowered and turned away and hid and made themselves scarce but didn't take the hint that they ought to get the heck out of Dodge.

Gilfgilf stood in a burning building and decided that there wasn't much he could do to save his folk, noble and polite as they might be. The best he could strive for was this: survive, escape from More of Them by the Sea, and plan to wreak a hearty revenge on the Bip-Citty forces.

And he would serve it cold, very cold.

It occurred to Gilfgilf that if he wanted to escape from the city, it was too late. All possible front entrances, back entrances, side entrances, and even secret passageways up and above, were blocked by nasty bloodthirsty killers. If he were powered to fly like a bird, they'd pick him off. If he bludgeoned a Bip-Citter from behind and took their uniform and tried to walk calmly out of town, they'd shoot him for deserting.

So he sneaked out.

So began Gilfgilf's quest for help into the unknown South, which would long be sung of (even today) in song and story.

Gilfgilf thought, *I won't get any help from the merciless, domineering King of Antwerp. East I might find help, for there live the crusty but good-hearted Green Forest Folk. To the North, I might find more help if I dared parley with the bad-ass toughies of the High-Steppes. Somewhere in this iodine-breathing planet lives the man who can organize armies; the one man who can speed my plan for revenge.*

The Lots of Trees Forest was the logical place to begin looking, but he didn't dare take the directest route there—East along Route 66. *The Bip-Citters would shoot me to electrons. I need to sneak, alive, 60 miles Southwest to the River Grunjy, at which, if I'm lucky, I can find a canoe or raft to carry me swiftly downstream to a point where I can trek East, to the Forest, unspotted at by Big-Citters, who call themselves Earthmen; but how best make my way the 60 miles to the river? If I follow Route 66, the enemy may catch up with me. After calm deliberation, I decided to follow the shores of Sea Ontheskale because that way I can keep an eye on the Bip-Citters, without them seeing me.*

Thus, did Gilfgilf lay his plans.

For four days, he followed the shores of the steaming sea closely, stopping occasionally to cook and eat some vegetables and barely in season seafood. Not until dawn of the fourth day did he hear the loud, brassy sounds of the Bip-Citters commencing their journey out of the city. *Bacchanalia,* Gilfgilf thought: *for three and a half days they've enjoyed themselves on the ravaged remnants of the once-proud, noble, and polite city.* Some three hours after thinking this thought, he came to the river.

He examined it intensively for some minutes, even to the point of thinking about taking a running leap across its nine-foot girth. Definitely, though, this river, which he had heard many stories about, but had never visited, was just plain weird.

He knew that the River had two ends: one at the shores of the Sea, one at the very bottom of the near-legendary BIG PIT. Surely, then, if the River Grunjy were following the Uranian laws of physics (as the educated D'Wharfs had known them), the River must begin at the Sea and run its winding 357-mile course downstream to the Pit. But the waters at this end were running upstream toward the lake.

Gilfgilf's plans were dashed. Enraged and disappointed, he kicked a tree in an ignoble and impolite way and hurt his foot. The pain brought him reeling back to his senses. *I'll cut down a couple trees and make a raft,* he thought. *Then I'll think of some way to ride the river downstream, even if it is going the wrong way.*

The hard, intense non-natal labor took him all afternoon. The distant sun was setting into the Krancky Mountains as he sewed the last beam of wood together. But, tireless in his determination and intestinal fortitude, Gilfgilf immediately threw the make-shift raft into the River, for he knew that the Bip-Citty forces were on the march, and there were no days to lose.

To his delight, the raft began immediately to float downstream, in contradiction to the River's conscripted course! Gilfgilf, who had been a careful student of physics in high school, soon puzzled things out. *The River Grunjy, rushing towards Sea Ontheskale, must leave a space behind it which the raft fills. This way I'm speeded to my destination.*

Gilfgilf, who had thought to pack a sack full of cooked

squirrels to eat along with his vegetables and barely in season seafood, was mightily impressed by the sights as he rode along. Birds flew, and fish swam, and branches grew. The sky, full of virulently poisonous gas, was a perpetual rainbow.

For three days he paddled to and fro with no incident. On the fourth day, he saw some gently-sloping appendages of ground: The start of the Mole Hills!

"There used to be a wise old saying in More of Them by the Sea," said Gilfgilf, making idle conversation to his dead squirrels, "It went something like, 'Nobody knows who lives in the Mole Hills.' Hmmm. I guess it loses something in the immediate translation."

As he rounded a busy corner, leading to a tall though widely-sloping hill, somebody said, "Put her up, Mein Herr."

Bravely though fearfully, Gilfgilf shoved his hands up.

"Throw us the dead squirrel bag, Mein Herr. There may be Euros in it."

Gilfgilf threw the bag toward the shore and then, just as instantly, dived headfirst into the River Grunjy .

He thought, *Ick! I forgot it was helium!* Spluttering up to the surface, he found three shotguns trained on his face.

Shortly, he found his arms tied around a post, facing a campfire.

"You don't us happy make, Mein Herr," said a voice belonging to one of his eight captors.

"You bring us no money and no pretty clothing, And no weapons besides a snapshot. And you don't have any currently-surviving uncle who's a king and can buy your ransom. Give us ten good reasons why we shouldn't kill you just for fun."

Gilfgilf gave much thought to this query. He finally settled on six reasons. "(1) It's not Christian. (2) The Geneva Convention of 2035 strictly prohibits such things. (3) It's a waste of your precious time."

"Ah, Mein Herr, we have all the time in the world. Even though it's a very small world, we have lots of time in it."

"(4) Because I'm so damn funny," Gilfgilf nothing daunted, continued, wagging his tongue, pitching a moon, and dancing "Top Hat." His audience maintained stony exteriors. "(5) Hey, fellas, I'm not done yet. Put those guns down, huh?"

"We are very bored, Mein Herr. When we get bored, we tie someone up, kill them, and then rape them."

All eight marksmen raised their Lugers, aimed with unerring, pinpoint accuracy at his brain, and fired.

Brave though he was, Gilfgilf began to sweat. As the situation grew tenser, a tall man, clad entirely in black, a black face mask even, riding a gryphon, and with a blazing letter "U" on his chest, rode into camp!

He drew a rapier from its scabbard and, swift as the very night, he stopped each of the soft shell bullets in mid-air, inscribing them with a "U." Then, dipping the point of the sword into a jar of red ink which he reserved for special occasions; he inscribed a large, bloody "U" on each of the gunmen's chests. They retired to the other side of the campfire to nurse their wounds.

"I apologize for the discourtesy of my men, M'sieur," said the dark-clad man.

"Si Vous play." Gilfgilf was surprised at the man's accent—was he one of Capped Anthony Spaulding's countrymen?

"Parley Vous min Langwej?" asked the man, slightly arching a disguised eyebrow.

"Sorry," said Gilfgilf. "I only learned Latin and Venusian in foreign languages. There was so much to learn in my highly cultured civilization that I gave up trying to learn it all and specialized."

"Bravo, Mon Cheri!" the man applauded. "Le Specialist! I shall speak, then, in ze common tongue of our planet, which we, like the Earthmen, call Uranus."

"Uranuse with an *e* and a diphthong," said Gilfgilf.

"Bah! I'll have none of your priggish More of Them by the Sea affectations," said the bemused man. Gilfgilf was surprised at his sudden temper.

"Okay. Uranus it is."

Half an hour later, after both of them recharged with hot squirrel shanks and a stoup of Miller Malt, Gilfgilf laid out his plans for revenge against the Bip-Citters.

"So how many Hill people do you think we can convince to take part in the war? And can I get a helicopter to take me to the Lots of Trees Forest quickly?"

"Neither, I am afraid. But if you get on your raft quickly and trust the current to speed you away, I think my folk will let you continue to live."

Gilfgilf was surprised for the third time at this masked man's mixture of niceness and hostility. What were his motives? Or did he suffer from split hemispheres?

As he sailed away, Gilfgilf saw the man, sitting splendidly on his midnight blue steed, smile and then scratch himself. Gilfgilf glanced at the handwritten note which had been pressed into his palm. It read, "Don't ask anyone for directions. U."

He passed through the Mole Hills without incident, although once a landslide caused by the Hill People shivered his raft in half and blocked up the River until, building into a torrent of hot helium, it forced the rocks aide; and once a three-hour machine gun volley barely missed the splintered remnants of his vessel.

Gilfgilf spent several days in lonely dejection. Would he meet with failure and hostility in all his efforts to organize an army? Would the flawlessly individualistic people of Part of Upper Uranus refuse to unite against a common enemy?

Days later he saw a lean, white figure coming towards him from the right. Could it be a friend? Probably not; but he slowed the raft and pulled it to the side of the shore to find out.

The man had long, flowing hair and a face that was not unamiable in the least. But Gilfgilf's experiences so far had made him very cynical. "Can I trust you?" he asked.

"Shore you can, Sonny Boy." Convinced, Gilfgilf told the man the whole tale of his adventures.

"So, anyway," said the last surviving D'Wharf, "I've come to a crisis point in my life. What should I do next?"

"Wah don't y'all come down to the Pompous with me, and we'll have a real good time? And whatevuh yuh do, Sonny, *don't go anywhere near* the Weird Marsh. Anybody does that is a damn fool and a Thug-lovah besides. Y'all come ovah to the Pompous, and we'll sit in the sun and make ya real happy."

The man's words were tempting, but he saw in them the same unprogressive, short-sighted thinking as had been displayed by the more urbane High King Celibate. Dead High King Celibate.

Gilfgilf made up his mind. "Which way to the Weird Marsh?"

"Just keep right on goin' the way you are—yuh horse's ass!" He heard the man leaning on his staff and laughing as he floated into the background.

Some fourteen or fifteen days after the destruction of More of Them by the Sea, Gilfgilf's raft drifted to the very edges of the Weird Marsh, which even the most advanced maps of Part of Upper Uranus labeled "Unexplored."

***

CHAPTER FIFTEEN

CAPTAIN'S LOG, APRIL 26 - (written by Lieutenant Harvey Baines Woofbanger): "O, I can't go on. No more; Nada Nada Na."

Captain's Log, April 25 - written by Security Chief Alf Simpson: *John Trawler's ded! I told the Captain she ought ta make Lt. Harvey Baines Woofbanger Ensin agen (do peple favors and then you can get em back sumtim) but she sad she wuz holdin the post open in onner of Dear Jonny for too days. Harvey Baines Woofbanger thot hed got the job so hes real upset again. He startid firing one ov the canons at our men, and we had to give him seda sedash saidati put him under for a while.*

"We enjoyd the fruts of our labors for thre and haf das eatin and drinking the stuf wed thougt ta sav wen we burned all ther billdings. The Captin she was real greatfil for me being so nice for avenjn her Jonny by killing evrybody in town so the Captain and I been having a real good time at night shes mitey compationit.

"After that we started out on are journey to the Big Fisher or something I forget what its kaled. One of the dwarffs said the Twerps lived ther and they wer the most powerful peple anybody's heard of cepting us. I ain't to worid about anybody lives in a fizure.

April 30 - Security Chief Alf Simpson again— "I shur hat riting. We ben having a lousy trip nothyngs goin rigt. 4 men (4) went catatonic from etin dex and washing it down with Moreathembythesee wine and we hade to carry them like two buy

83

4's. I wantid to leeve em were they were and let um wake up but the Captin she dont listin to me exxept in the bushes. That Commie pink-livered John Trawler put this help the wounded idea in her hed and she dont think strate no more. I say a man aynt grown up until hes slept off a good drunk on his oun.

"So heer we are carin these stifs wen six mor men did the same thing, and we have to cary them two. We took the wine away from them but they keep findin it. I think the Chaplens givin it to them on the sli. He's a Methadist.

"One good thing tho. There was a rare tropical bird flying overhead that one of aur men, a gooney named Benji Silverbeaster, lovs to collect. He was sayin 'A purplish Tuwange Belter! O Lord it's really here! For generations my family has traced the dim, obscure records of this bird, always thought to be mythical; but my family believed; we hunted on five continents; and to think I find it on the Planet Uranus! According to scrolls left in ancient Babylon there are only three of them alive in every century! To find one is to herald an era of unparalleled prosperity in one's family and one's nation.' So I shot the buzerd with my M-16. A few feathers fluttered down.

So now this Silverbeaster is catatonic too and wer'e carrying more men than we have to carry em.

Captain's Log, May 1— (written by Harvey Woofbanger): Ensign! I'm Ensign again; I can stop lying in my letters to Sis. She has a son to be proud of! By golly I feel good.

This in spite of the fact that we've wasted a good six hours of valuable hiking time trying—get this!—to get across a simple river! Our forces waded into the waters, only to be instantly wafted, rear-wise, back onto the shore! We tried extending a chopped tree across the grungy river and walking across it, but, no sooner had they gotten to the middle of the felled sapling, when the tree stood out of the water and sprung back to land! Several of our militia were stunned.

After several bad falls and some increasingly careful experiments, our ship scientist, Terence Hooker Cronwell, theorized a hitherto unknown property of liquid helium: 'The minute our men moved forward in the helium they left a space in the waters behind them, which the waters in front of them immediately pushed them back into (ibid, Vol IX, ps. 326-30).

Security Chief Alf Simpson, who had a very commanding personality coupled with a few rough edges, yelled, 'Come on you chili-livered expletive deleteds! That river's only nine feet wide; are ya men or do ya know how to jump across it?'

Somebody yelled 'Eat my shirts!' and Security Chief Alf Simpson shot somebody else dead. Several of the men wanted to lynch him, but the Captain, who has an appreciation for Security Chief Alf Simpson's finer qualities, said, 'He really is right, men. Jump across.' What was hard was the catatonics. We had to toss them.

On May 3, the Earth crew had been marching from ex-More of Them by the Sea for seven days. Brad McKray, taciturn, as always, and Joel McKray, jolly, told each other anecdotes to refresh each other's memories which, aided by dex, didn't usually reach further backward than fifteen minutes.

"Remember those three babes in San Diego, Joel?"

"Do I ever. Snap—*Shot!*"

"Where are the *broads* on Uranus?"

"We keep killing em."

"I haven't had one since *Cleveland!*"

"Hey, there, see the broad?"

"Joel, this is the second time you have attempted to pull the wool over my mind through joshing. You, sir, are the dumb straight man, and I am the jester."

"I mean it! Look at the broad."

Capped Anthony Spaulding, in a pretty summer dress, skipped along and sang, "Hullee gee, it sure is a swell day!"

Joel McKray and Brad McKray of the Earth McKrays, in very unison, yelled, "Let's get her!"

They sprinted for Capped Anthony Spaulding who, suddenly noticing their demented charge, prepared to knee them both where it hurt.

"Hey, Joel McKray, it's turned—it's turned—it's turned into a mushroom!"

"Say there, boys. Yo boys been seein' mushrooms?"asked Spaulding, who again wore his regulation private first class uniform, and who no longer resembled a mushroom.

"Capped Anthony Spaulding, haven't seen ya in ages. How ya been, ole buddy?"

"Not bad. I've been samplin' the simpler pleasures of life. Eatin' macrobiotic food."

"No stuffin? They bring macro food along on this trip?"

"Noooooo, homeboy! I grow it myself, as I walk along the briar path. It's simply a matter of mind over plant. Tell that there earth a few yards ahead 'grow macrobiotic food'—and it does! By golly!"

"Would you care for some herbal popcorn, M'sieu?"

Years later, Joel McKray would remember this as the most meaningful experience of his life.

The Captain, meanwhile, sat in her study, which was carried along by her adjutants, and questioned the purpose of their mission. Could it be, as John Trawler said, that their motions on Planet Uranus had been—inhumane?

What did the instructions (which he had never read) from Earth say?

She threw various items out of her cluttered dresser drawer: combs, autobiographies, memos, *belles lettres*. Then, in a gray envelope, sealed with red wax, in the sign of Aries, she found the letter, inscribed:

Washington, March 1st, 21st Century - These are your orders.

Should you decide to accept them, we hold no responsibility for the consequences.

Kill! Kill 'em men! Bang Bang! Kill!

Signed,

the boys

"No," the Captain said, "we've been following the right path after all. But Johnny's words come back to me."

No sooner had these words been uttered than the Captain heard someone screaming, "Fizzure ahead! Fizzure ahead!"

Soon all 6,983 ambulatory Earth people and eleven catatonics were assembled or propped up at a circular encampment, nervously, and the Captain began to address them.

"Well, men, we're gathered here in a democratic spirit to debate what to do next. According to reports we've gleaned from stray survivors, the Fissure of the Twerps is tops in both civilization and military power in this large part of the planet. We are at the extreme northern part of the Fissure; some 22 miles South of here and down under lies the capital, Antwerp, where lives the Big King Twerp, who, I have it on good authority, is the all-around toughest guy we have to deal with.

Now, as it stands, we have three main options: we can detour the Fissure altogether and continue our journeys Eastward without paying the Twerps heed. I don't need to tell you what I think of that," she said, sniffing haughtily and snapping her whip with its bolos down hard against the lectern, causing one of the rollers to spin off and the lectern to sag. "We can go in there with guns blazing and beat them into submission. Or," and she smiled, as a new light, even a heavenly, entered her eyes, "we can approach them with overture of peace and good fellowship. What'll it be, fells?"

Encouraged by this new familiarity from a Captain they had long thought aloof, several men made tracks for her, but soon died in them, as Security Chief Alf Simpson, Lieutenant Harvey Baines

Woofbanger, and other loyal adjutants potted them from behind cover. Security Chief Alf Simpson was nonetheless appalled at both the Captain's informal speaking, her calling of a democratic town meeting, and her monstrous third proposal. Peace and fellowship? With these no good, bad, foreign aliens? John Trawler might as lief be still alive!

"Well, uh, Captain," said a tall, lantern-jawed, lean-boned man from Maine, "I, uh, think, you know, that, uh, I kind of like Proposal 1. We've had enough, well, conflict for a while, but, uh, we don't really need to do any messing around with cooperating with these people. That would take years and then we wouldn't be able to file a complete scientific report and get back, well, to Earth on time."

"To Earth, yeah! Earth where ther'r broads!"

"Bring back Earth, Earth where there's broads!"

"Bring back babes!"

"Say, Captain," said a junior biology major at the University of Wisconsin, Osh Kosh, "I think that in listing all your speculated alternatives, you really left one of the alternatives out, you know? We could turn around and go back to the ship and take off for Spaceport Earth, okay? I sure have an urge to get back to the woods and go canoeing, myself."

Earth, Earth,
Quit the Mission,
Quit the Mission,
Give us Earth!

"Man, that's not a serious proposition," said the Captain. "We're not going back, so there. Now, can I hear some real debates on these issues?"

"The Captain wears a hernia!"

"Now that's no way to talk," said she, moved by her compassion to stay the enraged gun muzzles of her substantive armed guard. "We'll make the discussion simpler and narrow it down to two alternatives. Do we take the Fissure by force or enter it by niceness?"

"Sure, both."

Buy a goose and try to can it,
We don't want no seventh planet!
Give us Earth,
Give us Earth, (*in some versions of the text, this line is translated as "Earth no Dearth!"—Da Authors)*
Home of marrow,
Marsh and mirth.

"All right then, it's settled. We'll march into the Fissure peacefully, and be eager to be nice if they are. But we'll carry our weapons in our pockets just in case. See how well the democratic method works, men? We'll have to do it more often. G'night, now."

"This discussion ain't settled!"

THAT NIGHT BEHIND HER curtain, the Captain confided to Security Chief Alf Simpson, "I have a feeling, Alf, that the men are feeling disobedient. They might make a run back to the ship tonight if we don't stop them. But I'd rather not kill them all if we don't have to."

Security Chief Alf Simpson said, "You just rest assured that it'll all get took care of. I'll keep em in camp tonight and ready to march into the Fizzure. And there won't none of em get killed but aren't really asking for it." Smiling confidently, he stepped out of the tent.

An idea came to him.

Eight minutes later, Capped Anthony Spaulding mingled discriminately among the Earth ranks, agreeing with the men who were saying

"Hey, I've got an idea. Why don't we take off for the ship right now?"

"Yeah. It shouldn't take long."

"One, two days. How long has it been since we left the ship?"

"Yesterday? Can't remember that far."

Agreeing with them by saying, "Say there, my brother, why don you try dis here sheeyit. This stuff baaid!"

"Hey, there, cough, cough, cough. You certainly are right. This sheeut is, in the parlance of the street, bayad. Cough, cough; why thank you again."

Soon the entire Earth forces were stoned out of their gazebos. They suggested, "On with it, men. Let's run back to the ship. And double time it."

"That's right, homies. Run right back. This way. But don' go nowhere without your guns, yo, yo."

So it was that the Bip-Citters, armed to the teeth, and following Capped Anthony Spaulding's inaccurate directions, charged headlong into the Fissure of the Twerps.

"Is this the ship?"

"Why are we running downhill?"

"Sure is getting dark."

"What are those gray, darksome crenelations that run abaft the corners of this deep, pebble-be-strewn incline into which we run; and who those marksmen pointing their clubs at us? Did we take a wrong turn somewhere?"

So did the Earth ranks run into the unwelcoming arms of the mean and kill-crazed Thugs.

"Hey, man, we're under attack. Form ranks and kill!"

At this point, Security Chief Alf Simpson asked, "So, what's happening to the plan, then? What're our men gonna do when they get inta the fizhur?"

"They got a battle and a half on their hands, Sarge. In fact, they is sur-*ounded* 'bout now. Gnoamsayen?"

"You dumb mother-lover. I wanted ya to get em into the fissure, not get them dead. Come on, men, to the rescue!"

Motioning to the few dozen troops still outside the fissure, the chief military officer grabbed a Gatling elephant gun and leaped into the fissure.

Blam. Bang. "Ow." The troops shot several of the Thugs, but for every three Thugs shot, there were two others to take their place. The odds seemed discouraging.

Security Chief Alf Simpson ran into the thick of things, blasting anything that moved into jelly. Very soon the Thugs began to give him a respectful distance. So did the Earthers.

BUT THE BATTLE WENT on for lots of hours, but there weren't many fatalities because Ish, servant of the Big King Twerp, had promised the Thugs plenty more gold if they took their prisoners alive and in reasonably good health. And there weren't many Thugs killed because you can hardly kill a Thug. They're awfully tough.

"You should see it, Your Mass Entropy. The Earth dolts are getting their pants beat off. They should be ready to negotiate any day now."

"That's good to hear, Ish," said the Big King Twerp, who was even more glad of the opportunity to keep his telephone line busy for a few minutes. "Wait till they're nice and humble, then bring me their Captain."

"Sure thing, Chief. Hey, if you're bored, catch the 11 AM sports. I hear they got a new guy doing it with split hemispheres."

"Thanks, Ish. I might just do that. Bye-bye."

"By-dee wy-dee."

THE CAPTAIN WOKE UP in the middle of the night and reached for her favorite orange juice. She said, "I hear a lot of noise. But in the distance. Why are the men awake, and why aren't they here?"

Stepping out of the tent, she ran into Lieutenant Harvey Baines Woofbanger, asleep standing up.

"What's up, Lieutenant?"

"O Captain, my Captain! Gee, the men are all in a terrible battle in the Fissure. I considered it my duty to stay here and protect you."

"Good thinking, fella. Our men aren't having any trouble, are they? I mean, they are reaching a decisive victory?"

"I think so," responded Lieutenant Harvey Baines Woofbanger. "But it'll probably take them a few hours."

"Good deal. I can go back to sleep, then." And with that, the Captain spun about on her dainty foot and marched back into her tent to collapse once again in the arms of sweet Morpheus.

Capped Anthony Spaulding sat on the edge of the Fissure and watched things. He saw Security Chief Alf Simpson, standing in the midst of a large pile of dead and bleeding wounded. He was repeating the verb "Kill" in a vigorous monotone. He fired the last discharge from a bazooka, grabbing in the same instant a six-shooter from a pile of discarded weapons. He immediately re-commenced firing.

Brad McKray said, "If he keeps making 'em angry, the son of a bitch'll get us all killed."

"Shall we?" Joel McKray asked. They nodded at each other significantly.

Joel McKray picked up a rock and pitched it at the chief military officer. It took him from behind, and he keeled over rhythmically, as a log does. Joel McKray sniggered to himself for he thought he heard Security Chief Alf Simpson say "Gluhg?!" when the rock struck him.

The men, pressed valiantly, fought on for several minutes. Many of them had given up on the idea of damaging the Thugs with bullets and were now engaged in fisticuffs; but the Thugs, none daunted, continued to swing their clubs—when a club connected with a human's head, he fell for the count.

The bulk of the Earthlings, as was their wont in battle, were imitating corpses with varying measures of accuracy.

Time for me to take over, thought Capped Anthony Spaulding. He strode down to the middle of the battlefield, where Security Chief Alf Simpson lay, and shouted, "Peace, boys, peace! We conditionally surrender!"

Soon was their surrender affected, as Ish, servant of the Big King Twerp, mingled among the Thugs, reminding them that they'd only get their extra gold if they refrained from stomping on the prisoners.

***

CHAPTER SIXTEEN

GILFGILF INSPECTED HIS ROAD-MAP. "Yeah, this must be the Southwestern part of the forest. How do I find Genghis Twerp, though?"

He had come, by pain and travail, through the borders of the Weird Marsh; of his experience there, he would speak to no one.

His silent companions could give him but little aid, so he espied a hoary hermit and asked him for directions. The hermit attempted a saw-toothed grin and said, "If Genghis Twerp ye seek, paramour to the very Queen, go ye through that copse of trees and march ye straight for lots and lots of miles. Bunches, even."

"I trust him not," whispered one of Gilfgilf's companions. "See? He has a malicious eye."

"Yeah," said another. "He'll give a skull-like laugh if we follow his directions and get lost."

But, quiet as despair, Gilfgilf followed the path pointed to him.

After they had trod a little way, they noticed that the path was gone. Gray plain lay all around!

"Say, how'd we get into this country, it's pretty icky," one of his silent partners ventured. Cockle and spurge grew all about in place of flowers. The grass looked leprous; a wicked blind horse looked at them as they passed on. Gilfgilf's followers mumbled and threatened mutiny, but Nature looked at them square and true and said, "Ahhh, shut up, or shut your eyes."

Gilfgilf, trying to distract himself from this unpleasant and, in fact, impossible scenery, thought about past glories; but, nah, scandals and death and stuff—better this present than a past like that.

A little river ran by. "We'll have to ford it, men," said Gilfgilf, addressing, as was his wont, his followers.

Several shrieks later, they reached the other bank.

Gilfgilf, while surveying all the surrounding weapons of torture, saw his goal in the shadowed distance, but knew even then that he must, try as he might, ultimately fail. What the hell was going on? This had no continuity with his previous adventures, and he wasn't supposed to *have* any silent companions.

Suddenly, four tons of water fell out of the sky and squashed the universe.

"Say there, fella, we not let him have no more loco weed," said a voice in the shapeless darkness. Gilfgilf gradually realized that he was sitting around a lean campfire, accompanied by three of the brown-garbed Green Forest Folk. They looked at him with kindly, though freaked out expressions.

"You been thrashing around for eight Uranian time units, talkin' bout real strange things," one said. "Loco weed sposed to make you mellow."

As the clear light of sanity returned to his ears, Gilfgilf whispered, "I'm sober again. All's right with the world."

"Say, that's a real nice joke, boss. Now, why don't you a husha you mouth for a while."

Gilfgilf looked more carefully at his new friends. One, the one who had spoken, eyed him noncommittally. Another, who had blond, curly hair, openly leered at him. The third one, strangely hunched over, paced around the campfire, holding a suitcase and smoking a cigar.

"Say, you're the most ridiculous thing I've ever seen," said the cigar-smoking person. "I think you should know that they're about to tear you down and put up a puppy. If you don't like that, you can leave in a hut. If you don't like that, you can leave in a Uranian time unit and a hut. One thing, though. The squirrels are out for revenge today; you'd better duck."

"Vy should we a duck?"

"Oh, no, we're not going into that again. I suppose you'll want to know where you are and how you got here. But I can't answer that because I'm sad to say I must be going."

Gilfgilf looked confused. "Please stay."

"I'll stay a week or two; I'll stay the summer through, but there's a way, and I know that I have to go away."

To Gilfgilf's surprise, the other two Green Forest Folk began to imitate a train about to leave the station.

"Friends," said the man with the cigar and the suitcase, "no one who has never been placed in a like position can understand my feelings at this hour, nor the oppressive sadness I feel at this parting. For three-quarters of a century, I have lived among you, and never received a single kindness at your hands. But I don't need you; I can erect a taco stand. Friends, none of all, I bid you a fond and affectionate 'Phhhhht.'"

He climbed on the other two, who choo-chooing on hands and knees, soon disappeared into the trees; not before the leering blonde had pulled out a horn, honked it, and eaten it.

"What a bunch of stooges," said Gilfgilf.

Nonetheless, Gilfgilf's spirits were somewhat uplifted. He remembered that the part at the beginning of XV where he checked the road map had really happened; that several days had elapsed since then, and that he had traveled nearly to the middle of the forest. Any time now he should reach the small yet well-furnished clearing where currently resided the mighty and well-thewed barbarian, Genghis Twerp.

Suddenly, crude, harsh hands seized him from behind; a blow; and he again fell insensate.

"Should we kill him now, or bring him to Queen Rabid?"

"She has enough to do, what with her boyfriend and all. Let's kill him."

"We're taking him to the Queen because I say so. So there. Nyeah."

Thus, using many of the same democratic methods as the Bip-Citter's Captain, did they bring Gilfgilf before the Forest Queen.

"Who's the slug?" asked the Queen, whose custom it was to leave her tent—where she engaged in near-constant love-making with the much experienced but pretty tired Genghis Twerp—four times every twenty-four hours for a breath of fresh air.

"We knoweth not, humble and revered Queeny," they enjoined. "Probably some young punk revolutionary giving up city pleasures for the slothlier lifestyle and dangerously twisted rhetoric of some of the more advanced forest hermits."

"Oh. I suppose I'll have to talk to him, then. Slap him into sensibility."

This they did, and Gilfgilf soon found himself eying the one woman who stood in the way of his plans to save the universe from the Donkling invaders.

Their eyes met. But only briefly. Then Gilfgilf's eyes descended to a point lower than her shoulders but higher than her mid-riff. Queen Rabid's gaze lowered to a region somewhat below the feisty D'Wharf's belt.

"Hi there, handso—" she whispered dryly. "Men, take off. You've done thy job well good. If we need defense against this trifle, we can call on our big poopsie-woopsie."

The men parted, shaking their heads. "Hi there, handsome," she whispered dryly and throatily.

Forty-five minutes later, Gilfgilf picked himself up from the woman's somewhat flushed body. He stared into the strange tree-studded landscape of the forest. Above him, the spidery legs of trees stretched endlessly upward; a squirrel narrowly missed him with a rock.

"Well, I'll be," said a huge-thewed brute who eyed him with hatred and some respect. "Crod. You done went and laid Queen Rabid."

It could only be Genghis Twerp.

Queen Rabid lay face up on the turf with glazed eyes and a temporarily satiated look about the facial muscles.

Gilfgilf knew, with apprehension, that now he would surely die. "Gee, uh, Mr. Twerp, it isn't what you think it is."

"By Crod, you're joshing, son," he said, slapping his own haunch with delight. "But I don't know what it is a little fella like you has got, but whatever it is, you got it! She never passes out when I do it on her."

"No kidding? You aren't mad?"

"Heck, no. Take the bitch off my hands, why don't you? I've gotta get back into action, for only I can stop the Donklings from their vicious plan to—" He posed for added emphasis. "Conquer the Universe!"

"Actually, that was what I came to talk to you about. The Bip-Citters, you mean."

"Quit confusing the readers. Those who come from the third planet which we call The Great Donkey."

"Okay, the Donklings. Anyway, I think you're the only one with enough popularity and military experience to organize the Eastern half of Part of Upper Uranus into mass-resistance against the extra-Uranials."

"That's what I think, too. Trouble is Queen Rabid. She drains all my energies, saps my manhood. Right now, I probably couldn't even lift a little hairy elephant without a struggle."

"That bad, huh."

"Aye, by Crod and his demented hand maidens, aye."

"I can sympathize. You ought to drop her."

"It ain't that easy. If I make the Queen unhappy, she'll have me gelded and keep me on as a forest confessor. If I kill her, her loyal men in their grief will build her a funeral pyre and toss me on it."

Gilfgilf, who had read many romances, anticipated what the next part might be. G. Twerp would get an evil glint in his eyes and arrange things so that he could take off for torrid adventures while Gilfgilf got stuck living with the Queen. He took action to prevent this.

"I can do forgeries," he said. "I'll write out an imitation proclamation from the Queen, authoring us to take off for a year-long furlough and taking a large contingent of green-garbed men with us to the avoided North."

Genghis Twerp looked skeptical. "Can ye make an imitation that is passable?"

"Ink's ink. Besides, none of the Green Forest Folk can read. They'll fall for it like a ton of wet lead."

Genghis Twerp seemed willing to let him attempt it, so Gilfgilf started writing on a leaf, thinking, *Genghis Twerp can't read either, so I can write anything I want to, ha, so there!* He was wrong in that: Genghis Twerp, though unbrilliant, had a wide first-hand experience of many countries and could read and speak all known Uranian languages.

Gilfgilf wrote, *Dahling, I so enjoyed your book. Please do continue writing; but tell me, just between friends, was Lady Randolph's life really as scandal-ridden as you make out? And what about the second part, in America? Did an Indian visit her? And what about Naomi? Did her debut on Broadway pay off*

I really think the Lord should have stayed out of politics. He was consumptive, you know. Life among the classless societies was not as difficult as it once seemed. Please let me know when you bring out another. But really, dear, I think you should write the next one, don't you?

As ever,

Gertie

Genghis Twerp, poring over Gilf's difficult handwriting, said, "This stinks. It's not to the point. But we might as well use it, before the Queen wakes up."

Genghis Twerp prepared to call the forest people together and issue the royal proclamation.

"Say, there, uh, Gilfgilf, if that isn't being too formal, whatever it was you did to put the Queen to sleep, why don't you do some more of it while I talk to the men."

As Gilfgilf and the Queen remained sky-clad, he found this last instruction among the less complicated he had recently received. The Queen's glazed smile slightly grew.

"Hi, fellas," said Genghis Twerp. "Nice to see ya all again. Got a little message from the Queen here."

"Where is the Queen?"

"He's killed her. Kill him!"

"Cut it right off. Cut it right off."

"The Queen's just fine, old buddies. Got a little message from her here. It says:

Whereas we, the Queen, feel that our true and devoted love, Genghis Twerp, has been stifled too long by confinement to quarters, he should venture forth again into the world, taking along as many of the Green Forest Folk as will willingly accompany him and there do noble, useful and constructive adventures [from the bushes, the voice of one very like Gilfgilf, cried, Ah-Ah-Ah-]. In other words, most of you go with Genghis and follow his every bidding, even as mine; or incur my royal displeasure.

As ever,

Rabid

And P.S. I do so like motor cars, don't you?

"It's the Queen? Who else could write this?"

"I for one am persuaded."

"Ah— Ah— Ahhhhhhhh—"

"Tell you what, Genghis Twerp. The men and I have talked things over and have decided to do your every bidding. When do we start?"

G.T. thought of the Queen, who despite Gilfgilf's good efforts, might soon fully wake up.

"Start now," he said. "We can keep marching until I get tired. Straight Northwest with ya!"

Gilfgilf, whose powers of endurance were amazing for one so compact, was back on his feet, ready to march.

"Hi there, Gulfy, you don't mind if I call you that do ya?" said Genghis Twerp as they marched busily straight ahead, a strong thousand of them, leaving only the Queen and a few listless but loyal followers behind

Genghis Twerp felt much pleased by his new acquaintance. It was nice when he, a lonely leader of men, could have one guy he could trust. Kind of like Frank, whom he often thought about on those rare occasions when he recalled a need for male companionship.

The Queen soon finished waking up, but she was not overly peeved at Genghis Twerp. She had been thinking that it would do him good to get out and stretch his legs a little, though she had been unable to bring herself to part with him. Besides, if he didn't return soon, she had spies and subsidiaries everywhere who she could send out to kill him.

After nearly two days of marching, Genghis Twerp's forces reached the utter end of the forest.

MEANWHILE, IN THE KRANCKY Mountains, a child started going to day school and listening to stories around the campfire, full of thoughts far bigger than his surroundings. His mother had

101

passed away, and his father stared beatifically at a lone sheep on a faraway hill and thought of former glories, little knowing what was yet to come.

***

CHAPTER SEVENTEEN

THE UNIVERSE, LITTLE SUSPECTING what dangers threatened it from without and within, continued on its way. On Earth, the people celebrated 21st century science at a combined orchestra and light show.

One minister wept. "Best thing since Debussy," he said. He was the composer's father.

"Remarkable how they get both the sounds and the lights at once," said one old lady to another. Overhead, the city's skyscrapers stretched up for five, six stories.

The city grew on for four thousand miles. It contained a billion of the planet's best hearts and minds.

Everywhere lay—or sprang—advances. Elevated fire hydrants made impossible the prevention or cure of city fire. Chimpanzees, their personalities permanently boosted, sold popcorn (the return of the corner dime newsstand was one of the greatest blessings of the age). At one corner, an old codger, who thanks to longevity treatments, had reached his sixty-ninth year, glanced over the highlights of the official newspaper, and muttered, "Things could be worse. I really think so."

In the capital building, the President interrupted a busy day to think, *I wonder how the boys and that spitfire Captain of theirs on Uranus are doing?*

On Venus, the slow to anger Venusians jealously guarded

their plant sculpture, which early historic records said they had been designing for very near to nine thousand years. The Venerian culture is too complex to go into here, but they are a very peace-loving people who only wipe out entire planetary ecologies—such as the once verdant world between Mars and Jupiter—with mental blasts when totally necessary.

IN HIS PALACE AT Antwerp, the Big King Twerp awaited breathlessly for a phone call.

Ring. Brr-rr-ring.

"I wonder who that could be?" he said, running breathlessly up sixteen flights of cold, narrow stone stairs.

He picked up the receiver.

"Hi, BIG T. You don't mind if I call you BIG T, do you?"

"Good thing for you to say, but I'm waiting for another call."

"Hey! You can't talk to me like that."

"Go clean your dentures."

"Your uncle soaks his teeth too long."

"*Your* uncle made the seconding speech for Ralph Ryan."

"Why don't you make a speech at the Rotary."

"*O give me a home. Where the buffalo roam.*"

That was going too far. The Big King Twerp hung up. And they weren't really buffalo, either, they were bison. Idiot.

The phone rang.

"Ish here. I've got the Captain and several first officers here and can bring them up to negotiate if you feel so disposed."

"Good deal. I'll have to talk to them in the throne room, though. I haven't tidied up the tower in weeks."

The Big King Twerp, somewhat winded, descended downward.

PRESENT STOOD THE MOST important officers of the Fleet:

Security Chief Alf Simpson, Lieutenant Harvey Baines Woofbanger, the Captain—and Ensign Jedrey Spett.

"It's an impressive room," said Ensign Jedrey Spett. This despite the room having been despoiled of its gold weeks earlier by the avaricious Thugs.

"Lacks furnishings," said Lieutenant Harvey Baines Woofbanger, whose natural enthusiasm, pummeled by his experiences, had given way somewhat to finicky pickiness.

"All in all, though, not bad," said Ensign Jedrey Spett.

The Captain, who had grown more and more diplomatic since John Trawler's martyrdom, saw a dangerous argument impending. "Shut up, both of you," she said, stamping her tiny foot.

These preceding passages symbolize the internal agonies going on in the hearts of several of the characters, and their struggle to find an ethos in a world bereft of its multiplicity (*that should keep the English profs hopping for a few weeks, huh, kids?— Da Editors*).

The room's roof was stood hundred centimeters high. Painted on it were murals containing the adventures of all the previous Big Twerps (including Barney Twerp, circa 987-996, inventor of ceiling murals), most of them portrayed unfavorably. In fact, it was tradition for Uranian artists, proud and snootily independent, to subvert the honorary purpose of these murals. Only the current Big King Twerp's painted life story looked pleasing. He had put six painters to the wrack to get it that way.

The red crystal glass windows gave a broad overview of much of the Fissure, which was sooty and dusty and nothing to look at. The palace floors were built of marble, and mighty marble columns rose around the Big King Twerp's own dais.

The Big King Twerp entered the throne room, guarded by several armed Thugs (they had grown strangely placid since the battle five days earlier).

The Captain whispered to Ish, "Is this...?" Ish nodded. The Captain produced a genteel curtsy and, reaching for the Big King Twerp's hand, kissed it.

Security Chief Alf Simpson's natural patriotism was affronted. Were we going to be conciliating cowards to these cherry-hearted commie finko glad-handing aliens? To counterbalance the Captain's kow-towing, he waded through the midst of the Thug guards, punching their ugly guts and pasting them right on their warty noses.

The Thugs, while strangely quiescent, responded by aiming a couple of roundhouse punches at Security Chief Alf Simpson's solar plexus. Now he knew he was in a fight, and he loved it. *I coulda wished for sum help from them other tuna-hearted ofisers, but it looks like I mit havta carye the bal all bi miself for a wyl.*

The Big King Twerp said, "I am charmed enough by your gesture, Captain, for I take you to be a Captain by the commanding way you bear yourself, that I am willing to overlook this trifle on the part of your underling. Let you and I and those of your fellow officers who have a good attitude, repair to my dais where we can talk business."

Soon, the Big King Twerp sat in his throne, and the Captain, Lieutenant Harvey Baines Woofbanger, Ensign Jedrey Spett, and Ish, servant to the Big King Twerp, sat on the floor about it. Across the hallway in the background raged a big fistfight between Security Chief Alf Simpson and four of the Thugs. Outside, the First Mate *(whose "horse is the finest on Venus"—see CHAPTER 1)* beat against the guards outside protecting the palace and insisted that he, too, should be included in any top-level strategy conference.

"The situation, as I see it, is this," said the Big King Twerp. "You guys have shot your wad. We've got you surrounded and hopelessly outnumbered, and we took all your weapons away but are learning how to use them ourselves. You can throw in with my armies or get croaked."

The Captain tried a little bluffing. "Would you believe that the entire Earth Fleet is piloting to our rescue and will land on your palace roof in five minutes?"

"I find that very hard to believe."

"Won't go for that one, huh?" She batted her eyelids. "Would you believe that one other heavily equipped Earth ship, with my identical twin sister as Captain and hot for revenge, will land on your roof tomorrow with guns blazing?"

"Uh, uh. No."

"Would you believe one of our men is hiding a steak knife?"

"Let's get on to more serious business." The Big King Twerp moved in closer, his teeth glinting despite the piece of pimento still stuck between his xxx. "I am willing to negotiate with you on the terms of your surrender."

"You're leaving out one *important* factor."

"I am? Which one?" he asked.

"We left our ship manned at the Perfect Ambush Pass. All I have to do is signal the guard—our substitute science officer, very reliable—and the ship will fly over here with its lasers and pave this fissure into a smooth, glassy plain."

The Big King Twerp nodded significantly at his trusty right hand servant. Ish hopped to a panel in the wall and pressed a button, causing the ALL-SEEING EYE to slide out.

"Yes," the weary contraption responded.

"The UHF?" Ish asked.

The Big King Twerp nodded. "Yes, the UHF."

The blank screen coalesced into a picture: In the midst of splendid mountain scenery, slimy degenerate creatures crawled into an immense rocket ship. Soon after, the ship produced a billowing white cloud and rose upward into the sky, rising above the mountains and rising higher and pointing at the distant stars.

"My men are taking your ship back to your planet. To kill!

And destroy! And graffiti! (I like graffiti....)"

"Kinky," said Ish.

"And—and—ha ha hee hoo har har ho he ho ho heh," the Big King Twerp slapped his knees, rolled back his eyes and let loose gales of insane cacophonous laughter.

The Captain gritted her teeth and bit her lip. Her men had two feet in it now.

"Tell you what," the Captain said. "We'll do anything you want, as long as it doesn't go against our principles and our Prime Directive. What do you have in mind?"

The Big King Twerp himself stood up and pulled down the immense Map of Part of Upper Uranus, with which we are already familiar from earlier. *(Sit up and pay attention now!)* His eyes shook with idealistic lust. He said ...

"Power! These people stand un-united, ungoverned, their slothful lives backward and unproductive. Between the illiterate folk of the Steppes and the plump plantation owners of the vast Pompous there exists no desire to serve a single, beneficent government. (My tone softened and a piercing light of Reason entered my eyes, as I whispered, *my* government.)

"Only I, of all the people in Part of Upper Uranus, have enough dedication, education, and enough hobby horse sense to get these lands together, united, to build a technological civilization advanced enough to one day take over the entire planet Uranus. And then the solar system. And then, five years later, who knows."

The Captain, ever a hard bargainer, added, "So what do you need us for?"

"Your men have one thing that all my men lack—except Ish," the Big King Twerp said, patting the lad on the head and giving him a honey-flavored biscuit.

"Ooo, thanks," thanked Ish, munching happily on the baked morsel.

"Awareness. And you, Captain, and your best officers, have

a thing that in my continent only I and; and my arch-foe; possess – organizational sense."

"Ah, I get it. We help you conquer the planet and you build us a new ship to send us back home. Deal?"

"Sure. I want you to take the disorganized, lazy people of the Western half of Part of Upper Uranus and build them into a tightly-trained fighting unit, so we can conquer the East half. Start with...the Thugs."

"No sweat." The Captain clapped her hands and whistled to the four Thugs in the throne room, still pummeling it out with the ship's military officer. One of them turned around and said,

"Yeah, buddy, what do *you* want?"

"I've got a plan by which you can get a lot more gold. (*A man after my own heart*, Ish thought.) Go wash up and I'll tell you about it." The excited Thugs went to wash up. Security Chief Alf Simpson leaned against a stained crystal window, breathing hard.

"Excellent!" said the Big King Twerp. "But there is one element missing from my plan, one chink that permanently will not fit. I have reason to think that one of your men had come into possession of the ONE TRUE PORTY- PHONE, which, wielded by one as powerful and determined as me, would have made the mastering of men's minds a cinch. One John Trawler by name. I had counted on him bringing it to me. But your own men, led by that one," pointing to you know who, "*blew him up* and the porty-phone too at the palace at More of Them by the Sea."

The Captain was considerably put out. Turning to Security Chief Alf Simpson she said, "You knew he was in the palace when you blew it up? Oh, you cruel person." The Captain pouted, stamped her tiny foot, and pulled out her Walter PPK, shooting Security Chief Alf Simpson twice in the calf.

"And you," she said, turning to Lieutenant Harvey Baines Woofbanger. "What did you do to prevent it?"

"Uhhhhh," was his quick witted reply.

"You're relieved of your post, mister officer. "

"Nertz!" responded Harvey Baines Woofbanger.

"Ensign Jedrey Spett...."

"Yo, pretty mama!"

"You are now forthwith Lieutenant Jedrey Spett."

"Hot dog! Thank you, Ma'am."

"You're welcome, and you..." She turned to Harvey Baines Woofbanger. "Consider yourself an Ensign, Mr. Harvey Baines Woofbanger. Gentlemen, exchange pips."

"Yes! Ha! In your face, Ensign Harvey Baines Woofbanger, in your face!" Newly minted Lieutenant Jedrey Spett then proceeded to do an inspired little dance all about the room, singing, "Uh huh, that's right, that's right, uh huh, that's right."

Ensign Harvey Baines Woofbanger sank to the floor, foaming.

The First Mate sauntered in.

***

CHAPTER EIGHTEEN

GENGHIS TWERP STRETCHED HIS mightily thewed legs happily. "You know, Gulfy, by Crod, haven't been home in years. My people, simplistic as they may be, have an old, folky saying.'You haven't seen nothing until you've seen the Steppes.'"

"One thing you haven't told me yet, Genghis," said Gilfgilf, whose massive friend insisted that he (and he alone) call him only by his first name. "Are you a Low Stepper or a High Stepper?"

Genghis Twerp glanced at him with controlled disdain. "I am a *Stepper*. The people in the uppermost Northern regions persist in calling themselves 'High Steppers.' But I hail from the slightly more Southern regions; that is to say, the Steppes proper, by Crod."

A mist seemed to have fallen from Genghis Twerps's eyes since he had left the Great Green Forest. He looked as he had looked in his not-too-distant youth, a natural leader of men, a barbarian of few words, and even fewer direct reasoned thoughts, taking instant at the helm charge of any situation, not so much because of any particular talent or bit of knowledge (though he was long in experience and widely skilled) as through the sheer massive magnetic force of his personality. His biceps were the most massive anyone had seen. Indeed, two days earlier as they had neared the end of the forest, Genghis Twerp with several great swings of his hands had felled eight or ten decade-old willow trees.

111

The Green Forest Folk sensed this reawakening of his personality and deferred to him in everything, from tiddlywinks to Klingon opera. His wish was theirs to do. Indeed, had he told one of them to go take a running jump in the lake, the man had done it sooner than face Genghis Twerp's wrath and scrutinizing gaze.

"Better keep an eye out for trouble, men," said great Genghis Twerp in his resonant booming voice so that all could hear him for better emphasis. "Any minute now we're likely to get spotted by some border guards."

Even as he bellowed as unto a Uranian slack-jawed, mottled swamp beast, a battalion of some three dozen Low Steppers from a Steppe above them peered over the edge and growled with disapproval at the Green Forest Folk, fifty feet beneath them, led by an incredibly brawny and thickly muscled barbarian.

A somewhat older Stepper, who appeared to be the group's spokesman, said, "Genghis Twerp, why the consarned hayal did yuh want to come back for and bring an army with you? We exiled you as a lad of seventeen wintairs many years agoo for committing sodomy with unmarried air maidens, and for leading too many of oor valyeeable young boys on fatal expeditions to the ootlands. Since then, ye're every adventure, and there air many, (we subscribe to all of the pulp magazine accounts of thee) only fix in oor minds of confoormation of our greetest misgevings about ye. Adventure follows quest follows warfare follows adventure, and owleys evreyone involved except only thee ends up dead and perished."

"What the crack kind of accent is that?" asked several of the green-hued forest brotherhood.

Gilfgilf, who during their journey had been researching for the forthcoming authorized biography of Genghis Twerp and was thus probably more in touch with the facts than anyone else, said, "There is a saying among those peoples who have had to have dealings with these Northerners: 'No man's accent is so hard to pin down as that of the Low Stepper.' It is perhaps this very indefiniteness and idiosyncrasy about their pronunciation that long ago enabled Genghis Twerp to shake off all trace of any accent whatever and travel upon the word free and unencumbered by such a crippling cultural hindrance."

The old timer threw up his arms for added emphasis. "Drop boulders on him, men. And be swift to do so, y'all. Oi hev a predilection that if Genghis Twerp is permitted to live another 24 hours, he will leed awr youth to a wahr that weel result in the deaths of awl men in all nations. Even Genghis Twerp well dyy! So let him dyy now, by Crod, Myrtle, Mensa, and Mach-1!"

Genghis Twerp pointed at the old man, accepting his strangely accented challenge. "Chartis Pindarkin, I have waited many years for my return, so that I could extend a proper greeting to you."

So saying thus, Genghis Twerp hefted a mighty spear at Pindarkin, so that the haft of it bulged out of his heart, and the shaft of it stood out some three feet behind him.

"Ooey suppose you'll awl be wanting suppour and lodging, too," croaked the aged Stepper, who sank to the ground and died forthwith.

That night, for the first time in anyone's memory, Green Forest Folk broke bread with Low Steppers. And drank. This had been accomplished by Genghis Twerp's great personality and Gilfgilf's intelligence. But much more there was that needed the accomplishing than this truly historical cultural event.

"Most of you know me only through legend and various graffiti-like scrawlings on bathroom stall walls," Genghis Twerp said, wiping horse fat off on his gargantuan thighs. "Those of you who are a bit older may remember the time when, a lad of thirteen, I stole a sheep from Farmer Bill McGivney's farm. He said then, and told everyone to mark his words—"

"McGivney's dead these six years and thirty-nine days," a

grotesquely tattooed Low Stepper grunted while picking horse gristle out of his rotting teeth.

"Sorry to hear that. Truly." McGivney said, 'I'd whip the boy for this deed, had I not the sensing that he will one day be saving of all of Part of Upper Uranus.' I sense—nay, enough understatement, I know in my bones and in my loins—that that day is very soon to come. Did you folk mark an afternoon seven weeks past when an unusually bright meteor streaked out of the Western sky and landed in the vicinity of the Perfect Ambush Pass?"

"Aye, we did, verily, by Crod."

"That was no ordinary meteor. It was a band of lunatic emissaries from the Great Donkey, rowing an interstellar vessel to our planet to utterly destroy it."

"Oooooo! Ahhhhh!"

"Well advanced are their aims, these Donklings. Whole nations have died already by their cruel sweaty-palmed hands. But there is even worse in store; I fear: For the Donklings must eventually fall under the guiding grasp of the cruel, unnatural King of Antwerp. With their rapacity coupled to his inherent sinister wisdom, they will soon lay waste to *everything* and *everyone*.

"You have two choices: Join with me and as many of the free peoples as I can muster, or maintain your rustic ways and get squashed like unto vermin."

Moldo MacTavish, generally thought to be one of the shrewder of the up and coming generations of Steppers, tugged at his drooping Yosemite Sam mustache, and said, "Genghis Twerp, ye drive a haird bargain. But hoo air we to know that ye air noot making this all up, oor at least exogerating?"

Genghis Twerp thumped his chest with an equally massive clenched fist. "So a challenge to my word is it? Have I been gone that long? Well, Moldo MacTavish, you know as well as your father before you that there's one sure way of telling if a Stepper's lying or not." Genghis Twerp began to take off his white woolen shirt. Several Steppe women, seeing his huge hairy virile chest, swooned and fainted.

Genghis Twerp grinned at the young MacTavish. Moldo MacTavish, his face sweating, pulled off his own shirt.

The two men rose, advanced toward each other, and began to rub chests.

This went on for ten minutes, as everyone in the audience sat riveted in suspense.

Finally, they parted chests. An old woman in a gray bonnet ran her nimble fingers across both of their fronts. After long inspection, she said, "Thur's noot a hyeer follen oot of eitherr of therr chests."

"Then they moost both be tellin th' trooth," babbled the local village idiot.

Another pulled out clumps of his own long, greasy matted hair in bewilderment. "Acch. It has neverrr happened before."

Convinced of the honesty of his intention, and fired by his legendary prowess, a virtual horde, thousands even, of young male Steppers agreed to go with him into battle, even though it meant fighting alongside with the Green Forest Folk, whom they still found to be puny bean eaters. But the bad part was yet to come.

"Even the combined forces of these two free nations is not enough," said Genghis Twerp, after Gilfgilf's repeated insistence that he do so. "We must—be brave, men; we must join with the fighting folk of the so-called High Steppes."

"Tarnation and ill wishes!"

Many turned to one another, blathering on about old rivalries and various poor High Stepper hygiene habits.

"Do ye take us foor fools then, Genghis Twairp? We weel go in fairr adventurr, but noot for madness."

"Nay!" cried another. "We can only be one!"

"I'm not kidding," breathed Genghis Twerp, flexing his

mighty chest and arms. "Without them, our small-numbered forces cannot prevail against the Donklings. With them, we may pull it off. None of you can deny that those of the far Norther regions are fierce fighters."

"Suur they be fairce fighterrs. Papists are allways fairce fighterrs."

"We'll noot throw in arr lot with an arrmy of rabid Catholics."

Genghis Twerp's own sympathies were so essentially in agreement with this that for a while he was at a loss for what to say. Gilfgilf slipped him some notes, and he went on, pacing as he spoke around the blazing community fire. "Give me none of your errant provincialism! If Big King Twerp of Antwerp takes over, you'll have no freedom to practice your Calvinism. You'll not even have local control of your schools!"

"No local controwal of the schoools?" asked an old Stepper, deeply moved.

"Parhaaps, then, wee should reconnsiderr, after all," reasoned another.

But, Gilfgilf learned by a quick random sampling of the Steppers gathered round the campfire, the vast majority of them were still unwilling to join the High Steppers in much of anything, especially in orchestrated military maneuvers. So, at his signal, several of the Green Forest Folk went among the multitude distributing their special, tree-grown loco weed. Soon, a veritable horde of jolly fighting men, pikes in hand, began the arduous climb to the High Steppes.

They climbed all the way that night and, just before dawn, fell and slept like unto the very logs all day. As they were motionless, the High Steppers failed to notice them.

They woke in the late afternoon and quickly jumped to their feet.

"Hoot, Mon! Do I see an array of filthy haiethen baptists?"

"Get on with ye, Arnie MacDougal. Nary a low-stepping Protestant has crossed these borders for upwarrds of thray generations."

"Ye have a point there, Holly McGinnis. Still, if my ayes d'nay mickel decayve me, the veriest throng oov unwashed pagans stands dayrectly beneath us."

Gilfgilf said, "Better use the direct method before they get their bearings."

Mighty Genghis Twerp, who gave much weight to all the words of his friend, stood up suddenly and said, "I am Genghis Twerp. My friends and I come in peace. The Pope is okay in our book."

"Oh, so it's convayrsion ye want?" said a priest who sprang from his passionate embrace with a High Steppe lassie, ready to do his duty for any misguided person requiring salvation who stumbled upon his jurisdiction.

"We seek not conversion, but cooperation. Both our nations must unite against a common foe."

"It be eld n' established coostum in th' Haigh Steppes that a Haithen intairlooper eithairr excepts conversion, or accepts death." So said a brawny shepherd in a plaid miniskirt.

"Well, if it isn't Bertie Graeme!" said Genghis Twerp. "My drinking buddy these eight springs past."

"Aye, that I be, ye unshaven goat plonker, aye, that I be."

Genghis Twerp clapped his mighty hands together and bellowed, "Men, wheel up the vat."

Promptly, the Low Steppers and the foresters wheeled up a thirty-foot vat of Low Steppes wheat juice and, sending five pike-carrying heights-forders to pull and chop their way up the last Steppe to where the Catholics stood, they secured the vat with ropes, and the first five climbers began to haul up the killer vessel. Their veins bulged and their muscles strained, for it was monumentally heavy, but they were Steppers, so the task was not beyond them.

The dozen or so High Steppers who had wandered by to watch the proceeding regarded it with a morbid and almost superstitious fascination.

Soon, thousands of god-awful drunk High Steppers were slapping their Low-Stepping buddies on the back and extolling the virtues of paganism.

***

CHAPTER NINETEEN

AFTER THAT, THINGS HAPPENED very quickly. It seems appropriate, before getting into the part of the story which will probably result in the destruction of all of Part of Upper Uranus, and the kindly folk living there, to give a brief overview of some of the lands and the people, and tie up twelve to thirteen loose plot ends. We don't want you to think that we authors didn't think our plot through enough.

An author's life is an unrewarding life. You spend four hours a day hunched over the typewriter or squinting at a portable computer screen, tap-tap-tapping away, and what do you get for it? Money, I ask you, is that fair? You readers lead a much more fulfilling life. You lean back and read a good, racy magazine, and you get to *shell out* money for it. That gives you a sense of accomplishment and satisfaction. Where is the satisfaction for a writer of Romances? If we were doing research for a biography of honest Ronnie Reagan, there would be some satisfaction, it is true, but what happiness is there for a fella (the Romance-writer) who makes his career out of writing lies?

A careful examination of your map will tell you that so far your plot action has only focused on *part* of Part of Upper Uranus. What of the Vast Glass Lands in the far East and Gnorway in the Northeast? Don't worry about them just for now. You're a professional. You'll get to all of this in good time. What of the

Wizard's Tower and the Weird Marsh, which we pimped you by skipping over when Gilfgilf got to it? Just hang tight. Right now, we can tell you that the Wizard's Tower, from where the Big King Twerp and other TV watchers to the West got a lot of their valuable information, was the home of the Wizard, who was the legitimate son of the aforementioned evil wizard Jasux, so you can guess rightly that he knows something about the whereabouts of the ONE TRUE PORTY-PHONE.

While we're at it, and because we can at the moment, let's take a tour of his lab. It's Saturday morning at 11 AM, and he's beginning a new episode of his weekly TV series that just came out of reruns and a very intense letter writing campaign to keep it on the air.

"Billy, today I'm going to learn you all about mercury." *(Produces a thermometer and smashes it over the child's wrist, then pours the contents on the table)*

"Gee, Mr. Wizard, Sir, you mean mercury isn't red?"

"No, it ain't. It's silver. Mighty *quicksilver* too." *(Winks at the TV viewer.)*

"Mr. Wizard, boss, is it true that mercury is the only metal that is liquid at normal room temperature?"

"That is true, sonny boy. If you keep in mind that Uranus's room temperature is distinctly *ab*normal. Stick this outside on our planet for a few seconds, and it'll be solid like everything else."

"Mr. Wizard, is it truly true that you are really God?"

"No, Billy," (fingering his empty pen pocket with remorse) "Not yet. No, sadly, not yet. But soon, very, very soon."

He stifled the urge to throw his head back and go, "Mwu-huh-huh-huh!"

THE CAPTAIN HAD A lot of organizing in front of her before any decent war could get started. She soon learned that the naturally anarchistic Thugs were almost impossible to organize; if she gave them instructions they would carry them out if they felt like it and not do so if they didn't. Through this haphazard method of training, they learned the meaning of basic rudimentary military discipline, and how to respond to all the different orders—if they all felt like any of it, of course.

While the Captain was telling the Thugs where to go, a military expedition led by Lieutenant Jedrey Spett and Heinlein, the new military officer, and including Capped Anthony Spaulding, Brad McKray and Joel McKray, and five hundred other Earthlings, marched many miles through the Fissure until they had deeply penetrated into the Concrete Jungle, whomsoever inhabitants they also intended to annex into the glorious cause of war.

Of Lieutenant Jedrey Spett and Heinlein, we have little record. It may perhaps be said with accuracy that their personalities tended more toward the median, and were somewhat less colorful than some of the other corkers whose adventures we have been describing. As newly made important officers they were promoted from the black to the executive red dex, which, though clouding their abilities to question anything that the Captain said, left their minds reasonably clear otherwise.

Heinlein, born of a poor family and a thoroughgoing proletarian, much less likely than the wounded, disgruntled Security Chief Alf Simpson to shoot one of his men for sport, mingled among the troops and exchanged ribald pleasantries with them.

"Say there, Joe, is that a picture of your mother?"

"Nah, Mommie's too old to pose in one of those, Heinlein," said the aforementioned Joe.

"One of what's?"

"Hey, that was pretty funny. Did you hear the one about the drunk sailor?"

Lieutenant Jedrey Spett, holding his eyes up, said, "This

fissure really gives me the creeps. I'll be glad when we get out of it."

A few men carried torches. Otherwise it was dark. Ish said, "The folk of the Fissure are all blind."

"How'll they be any good when we get to fighting?"

"Just watch."

Now that John Trawler was gone and Security Chief Alf Simpson demoted, Capped Anthony Spaulding now was temporarily left without anyone he could influence. He kept mostly to himself, mumbling French ditties.

Then it occurred to him that if he could gain the ear of Ish, servant to the Big King Twerp, he'd be only a step away from controlling everything. "M'siuer," he said, quietly, "what are your motives in serving ze MAN? What can du gain from it in ze end?" Capped Anthony Spaulding twirled his imaginary curly black mustaches and arched an eyebrow significantly for emphasis.

Ish said, "I ask myself that sometimes, too. I think for thrills mostly. I grew up in a moldy barn where my only playmates were pigs and cretins. The common life ain't no pizzeria, I'll tell you. Through diligent habits and doing my arithmetic with chalk on a shovel, I gained the equivalent of a fourth grade education. Then, when His Mass Entropy announced a civil service examination, I took it, and since I was the only one in the Fissure besides His Mass Entropy who could read nor write, I naturally won and got the job. There are those who call me illiterate and ascribe all my ideas to one Burroughs. But they are sadly and woefully mistaken."

"But what about *Loung destance*, what we Franks call ze Long Run? Does it never occur to you, M'sieur, that a man of your native intelligence and character could 'have le big cheez,' could rule everything yourself? You are too good for a mere servant."

"You've got a point there. I never thought of that."

Capped Anthony Spaulding thought, *He weakens! Soon, soon, he will be my slave! Muh-ha-ha-ha!*

Ish interrupted their conversation to announce the

following: "We've come far enough, pards. Time to climb up to the jungle."

The Concrete Jungle was miles and miles of natural rock formations, mixed with statues and buildings and trees that looked like they were indeed made of concrete. Whether they were really concrete or not, no one knew, since no Uranian civilization had probably had enough technology to mix the stuff. But they all looked like concrete, so they called them that.

As the men, somewhat mortified by this stupefying sight, wandered around stoned through this jungle, they saw lots of inhabitants. Concrete lions. Concrete tigers. Concrete bears. But was there anything...alive?

Lieutenant Jedrey Spett was, all things considered, not a bad choice for Ensign. He had some reasonable faculty for decision making coupled with a healthy and great respect for others' opinions. Handsome, in a lean sort of way, with dark hair, and he wore a neat gray knee-length trench coat. He asked, "Ish, what do you know about the people of this jungle?"

Ish said, "They're very shy. But if we keep combing the area, we'll poke some of them up."

Suddenly, he came! Swinging through concrete trees by concrete vines! Wearing only a green loin-cloth (geez, what you could see under it in breezy days). Knife in his teeth! A savage tremolo issuing from his noble savage lips, announcing his advancing brachiating fury. Ready to kill, and kill, and kill, until his people were avenged their loss of privacy.

"All right, I hope you know you're performing three misdemeanors," he said, writing in his notebook with his ivory-edged knife. "Loitering. Trespassing, and assembly without a permit. You got anything to say before I deliver you your notice?"

"Heck with you, Pig," said Heinlein, who, as one of the People, had had to deal with his arrogant kind before.

The stranger was taken aback by this. "I guess you're right; I

123

did introduce myself a bit too formally. I am Krako Natzar."

Ish said, "We'd like a little friendly get-together with your people, if it isn't too much of an inconvenience."

Nodding affirmatively, Krako Natzar put his fingers to his lips and blew. It was above the level of human hearing, but, back at Antwerp, Benji Silverbeaster was shocked out of his coma and sat up, blinking.

Soon the whistling got its response. Sixty urchins wearing concrete jackets, even the young females wore them, appeared from behind various rocks and converged in a couple of semi-circles around Krako Natzar, bobbing up and down.

"Blimey!" said an older one of them, perhaps a male about thirteen. "Whatta you want now, Guvnor, eh?"

Krako Natzar thumped his chest. "Prissy little lad say 'hi' to nice mans. They friendly, besides, they got plenty firepower. Ko-gala."

"Cor! Don't give us no more Elmo Lincoln jive, mate. Blimey, we all know 'at you were raised on a concrete plateau by a tribe of now-dead great white giraffes after your folks abandoned you there. But yore thirty years in Parliament rightly well countered your rude up-bringing a long time ago."

"What a flock of bright ones!" said Krako Naztar, beaming. "Can't pull a thing over on 'em. I tell you it'd go hard on the old man to lose one of 'em."

Lieutenant Jedrey Spett said, "Maybe this isn't the time to talk about conscripting your whole nation into deadly, bloodthirsty war, then."

At the mention of danger to his kids, Krako Zatnar's reaction proved instantaneous. He pulled his knife out of his teeth and thrust at the heart of the nearest Earthling. Fortunately, he missed.

Later, after some forty-five Earth troops held mighty Krako Naztar at bay, while the urchins looked on in amusement, and while Dr. Bidge Chetterton, the ship physician ("Dammit, I'm a doctor, not a veterinarian!"), pumped him full of 90 cc's of sedative, they discussed the matter like mature adults. "Look at it this way," said Heinlein. "I sympatize wit yuz. But, heck, shoot a mile, it'll keep them kids off the streets."

Krako Zatnar's noble savage face blazed hatred and defiance and unsettled disagreement. "No dice," he said.

While this was going on, the youths were busily circulating through the Earth forces, checking the wallets and discarding the ones that weren't loaded enough. "Rats!" little Jethro whispered. "Army guys make more dough than this. Did they go and spend it all in the pinball machines?"

Brad McKray and Joel McKray, oblivious to the fact that their life savings were being robbed, studied the many interesting shapes that the rocks had taken. "Say there, Brad McKray," said Joel McKray.

"Say there," replied Brad McKray.

Joel McKray continued. "I have heard the rumor that the spaceship got destroyed and we'll never get home again?"

"That's just an exaggeration. A bit of misinformation, propaganda, if you will. Hey! See that moving stone lion over there by the hills?"

"What? What? Where?" In his frantic urge to escape, Joel McKray fell over, thus temporarily saving his wallet from the grasp of a greedy urchin.

"Just a josh." Thus, Brad McKray put Joel McKray back in his proper place as the fool to his straight man.

A stoned vulture flew by in a hurry. "A buzzed buzzard buzzed busily by, buster!" cried the Chaplain, pointing. Very few paid him any heed.

"Be humane, men," said Krako Natzar, "be sensible! These foundlings can't be cut off or down in their impressionable youth., never to see the ripe dawn of adulthood? I've worked hard to bring

125

up these kids properly after they let me out of the slammer. I made up for my former misdoings by raising these orphans from burping babyhood to bouncing cusps on the verge of adolescence."

The urchins began to draw out their bicycle chains and swing them. If one of them connected with an Earthmen's skull, well, that was too bad, so sad.

"Brought 'em up good, I tell ya. Those kids are a wonder, I tell ya. I taught 'em healthy games, and I taught 'em always to respect their moms and the home country. I taught 'em the Constitution and the Ten Commandments and the alphabet."

Dissatisfied with their previous haul, the youths turned to active mugging. The Earth fighters, seeing a knife pointed at their ribs, started to scream for help, but didn't when they saw the knife pointed at their neck. This haul was somewhat better, gold watches and jade frat rings and Mickey Mouse watches and such.

My example speaks for itself." Again Krako Nazrat thumped his mighty chest (possibly for emphasis, although it was quite possible he just liked the sounds and sensations of chest thumping...) I ask you, friends. I take you to be decent men. Do you send these bobbins to a horrible death, and they'd be no good as fighters anyway—or do you let them grow up into healthy, well-bred citizens and servants of the Republic?"

The heavy-jacketed adolescents, beginning to grow angry at the large number of unwealthy Earthmen, began to prank them.

"Tell you what, Krakonats," said Heinlein. "We won't make em come except those that want to go. But why don't we tell em their options and if they want to join, they can?"

Naratz started to argue again, so they pumped him with 300 more cc's, enough, said Dr. Bidge Chetterton, to put him "under for a week."

Lieutenant Jedrey Spett clapped for the kids' attention. When he told them that they could join the army and fight for the cause of Earth, the boys all ran away, but the girls, some thirteen in number, opted to stay. They calculated that sixteen-year-old girls wouldn't be made to do the harder fighting, but might mostly be kept to labors more fun and profitable. Sick of the priggish, pre-pubescent lads of the Concrete Jungle, they looked on to find glory and commercially marketable skills that would one day prevent them from going to trade school that only advertised late at night on television before the infomercials took over.

THE PEOPLE OF THE Krancky Mountains are few and far between. They are fiercely independent second in their obsessive demand for individualism only to the Thugs. One of them, depressed and upset because he's misplaced his coffee money, reached for a nearby telephone.

WHEN JOHN TRAWLER AWOKE in a cave in Northern Arizona, he saw his naked dead body lying on the ground beneath him. He looked out of the cave mouth and saw that the Indians were gone.

He went back to his Pennsylvania plantation and remained ageless. When many years had gone by, he stood alone on the veranda with his wife, Elizabeth, and looked in the general direction at the cool blue distant orb of Uranus.

"Are you going to the East Room tonight, Richard? I see it in your eyes."

"I *am* going to the East Room, Elizabeth. Will you come with me?"

"Not this night, Richard. But I will, someday."

Bidding her adieu, he went to the East Room and looked at the planet. It tugged at him. Even as he felt his heart drawing its last few beats, he gasped, "Uranus, I'm coming back."

***

CHAPTER TWENTY

GETTING THE STEPPES TOGETHER proved un-easy. Every time the two nations got ready to sign a treaty of co-operation, someone came up with a new niggliong objection.

"I like this coupperration noot at awl," said Bilko MacBake of the Clan McBake, an old and much respected High Stepper. "If wee sign a traity with you, you'll be pushin' yare oon rigid ways oon us. Wahrke awl day, goo to chairch all Sunday, end no tiame forr the lassies."

"That's just it," Tommie McKravish of the Clan McKravish, a young upstart Low Stepper, said. "You Papists'll bee hevin us populatin' all the time. We'll not be able to roam in the gloamin' withoot trippin' ovar hooards ov child-makers."

"Awl thet you Calvin lovers know what t' do is ways oov makin' money. Ye give a Hooy Stepper money, and hay rightly knows how to spend it."

Gilfgilf had for the most part been taking only a covert part in the negotiations, but this constant bickering was sorely getting to him. "Come off it, will ya? You don't have to live together, you're not asking one another to sign off on a loan, either; just to fight a big war. Then you can come back and continue your old ways just as close-minded and persnickety as ever."

Moldo MacTavish of the Clan MacTavish said, "I like yer reasoning, man of the sea-shore." Since learning that Genghis

Twerp was honest, Moldo MacTavish had come more and more to favor their side of things.

Moldo MacTavish would be some twenty-three years of age by Great Donkey reckoning. He had considerable influence among the younger, abler members of his race; and when he talked up co-operation with the High Steppers, those who were not yet old enough for experience to confirm their prejudices agreed with him.

What was needed was an influential youth on the High Stepper side to join his arguments to the common toil. She was found in the person of Shanie Lola McBrideburgh of the Clan McBridgeburgh, a buxom lassie of seventeen winters; a virgin, and a fierce, though genteel, hunter—and a wildcat fighter when her kinsmen were threatened. The story was still told how a roving band of marauders and plunderers had skirted their borders (led by Genghis Twerp, but he had been in disguise at the time and he kept quiet about it when he heard the story mentioned) and Shanie Lola McBrideburgh, a chit of fifteen, had run buck-naked at the invaders waving a thick stalk of heather, and they, thinking her some mythic demon goddess, had fled in terror. Now she said, "Noot for nothing wawld aye advise ye men of different Steppes and different worships to warak teegether. But noo ye have a choice of living tagether long enough ta get a warr finished, or dyin togather oonder the hard brick bow of the Big Twairp. Do yee noot feel moowr kinship for a Stepper of any stripe than fair a Donkling or a Thug?"

"Hear! Hear!"

"I kent with awl moy ain it is so."

Gilfgilf saw that the tide of opinion was turning favorably, but the mass of folk needed more convincing. He walked up to Shanie Lola McBrideburgh in her cute tam o' shanter and serenaded her with a bag, which action she seemed rather to like.

"Huzzah! Huzzah!" yelled the Steppesmen, who were now even more inclined than ever to sign the treaty.

129

"Besides," yelled Chonk McBogning of the Clan McBogning, a High Stepper, "therr baritone bag-playing goes weel with oor tenor!"

This conclusive argument proved convincing, and they signed the treaty almost instantly.

During all of this, the Green Forest Folk, rather bored and growing complacent, had been practicing the art of bag playing, which on Uranus is accomplished by blowing into a blue paper shopping bag until you get tired and then letting the air run out.

AFTER EXPLORING THE CONCRETE Jungle a while longer, it was discovered by Lieutenant Jedrey Spett and company that not all the inhabitants were kids. There were also a goodly number of winos, pimps, role-playing gamers, roller derby girls, and insurance salesmen. When some of these had volunteered or been conscripted and added to the thirteen young female volunteers, the army found its ranks swelled by some forty-five.

ISH HURRIED BACK TO Antwerp in time to join the Captain in an expedition to the Land of Thug to recruit some more Thugs. This proved largely unsuccessful, since most of those Thugs who were willing to regimen their normal anarchistic, day-to-day living long enough to engage in a concerted hunt for gold, were already *in* Antwerp. By promising them a dinner of live gnome-meat in the Lots of Trees Forest, Ish was able to persuade some five hundred more Thugs to join them, 275 of whom actually followed them as far as the Fissure.

On the way back, they stopped off at Sing-Sing, on the beautiful Western shores of Sea Ontheskale.

Strangely, this land was not inhabited by singers, but by horse breeders. They were in the midst of a derby as the Captain and company marched through.

"Awsamanawellotmapquallookatemgowangdofnicksobsobi

chbyacountrymile," wailed the loudspeakers in this small, out of the way sleepy hamlet with its uniform green roofs on every building, whatever shape or size.

The balding city clerk looked up from his papers and blared to the Mayor, "HeylookChieftherestourists!"

The Mayor, a young fella elected forty years earlier on a reform platform, woke up and slowly sat bolt upright. "Sureyou'renotjustseeingthings?"

"Nothere'stourists.Seeallthemguns?Theyvecomeheretohunt quail."

"Betterbreakouttheband,then."

The Sing-Sing inhabitants, always glad to have visitors, ran up to the military entourage and greeted them in their native tongue. The Earthmen were perplexed; it was their first encounter with a foreign language.

Suddenly, the Sing-Sing high school marching band appeared in the middle of the street in front of the invaders, wearing their red suits and blowing their tubas. The Thugs were terrified. They ran at the students with their sturdy clubs and began knocking them down like bowling pins.

"Heycutthatoutyoucantgetamotelhereifyoudon'tlikeSouza."

"Ifyou'dliketogetstartedwiththehuntingtherearequailintheal leys."

"What do you think, Ish?" the Captain asked.

"Let's level the place."

The Captain put a bullhorn to her lips and stood on the court-hall steps. "In fifteen minutes we're going to start shelling your town. If you want to live, you can join the army of the mighty King of Antwerp."

The Mayor smiled and put his arm around the Captain while the city clerk took a picture for the bi-weekly town newspaper. "Martha,haulouttherootbeer," Farmer John whispered.

ON THE FOURTH DAY of their march, the Freedom Fighters of Genghis Twerp arrived at the ancient, shattered barricade between Them and Us. Moldo MacTavish and Gilfgilf and Shanie Lola McBrideburgh, and Ralph Shockmead of the Green Forest Folk Brotherhood had been appointed a quadriad by Genghis Twerp to negotiate with the two bruised city-states. Genghis Twerp reasoned that these people might still be touchy about his little altercation with their children in the Perfect Ambush Pass. His presence might be counterproductive in the preliminary stages of negotiations. So he had taken a few picked killers from among the Green Forest Folk with him to the Krancky Mountains, hoping there to drum up a steam of anti-Big King Twerp fervor.

The peoples of Us and Them, whose mature social structure had prevented warfare betwixt themselves for hundreds of years, had now grown actively hostile toward any more outsiders carelessly and imperially messing with that social structure. They waited for the Freedom Fighters at the former barricade, with guns and knives and staffs and pitchforks and bazookas. Some even carried heavy rocks. Very heavy rocks.

Genghis Twerp stood on a rocky crag and looked about him. Life in the mountains, it was free. A cool breeze, almost like a sea breeze, stroked his jutting stubbly chin.

"By Crod, see any Mountain Folk, men?"

"No, your headness, and we're not likely to, neither. I hear tales from my grandpa that these mountain lovers make themselves scarcer than common sense when company shows."

Adjusting his power tie, Genghis Twerp said, "I'll give an after dinner speech. There is nothing a Mountain Folk hates more than an after dinner speech."

His three companions settled into folding dinner chairs. One of them tapped his glass with a *spoon of chiming.*

Genghis Twerp parted his hair for emphasis and began. "Friends; fellow citizens—uhh— Gee, I'm not good at these. Could you give it, Julius?"

His brown-garbed friend of the forest brotherhood rose to the lectern and tapped out his cigar on a nearby rock. "Friends, you're very happy to see me tonight. Unfortunately, I can't return the compliment.

"Where was I? Oh, I must go mad. The topic tonight is government. Government! Where would we be without it? And whatever can we do with it? Go to the back of the class." Julius smiled, pointing at a rather handsome brunette standing by the water cooler. "And you, young lady, see me in my office after my speech.

"Government helps us to do what we should be doing, instead of wasting our time doing what we want to do. And who is it that will help us all abandon our pleasant woes, and become happy, fulfilled citizens? The Big King Twerp, that's who."

A crowd of squinting, unshaven Mountain Folk had begun to assemble.

"Government will light your campfire, and you, shorty, it will buy a used pair of glasses. What you'll use them for I won't care to know. With a Thug cop on every corner, you won't have to steal marbles or spit into the wind. Try Big King Twerp brand, okay in your book or mine."

Some brown-garbed person in the audience yelled, "The Big King Twerp, he a stink. You gotta da fresh haddock so we can drown him out?"

"Yeah!" yelled Mountain Folk from all around. "The Big King Twerp! Let's hang him until it hurts!"

A blond man with shears ran about the mountain slopes, cutting people's suspenders, laughing soundlessly.

Genghis Twerp, rising to the fore, yelled, "That's right. Let us show the Big King Twerp what he can do with his government. Give me a 'K,'"

"K!"

"Give me an 'I.'"

"I!"

"Give me an 'L.'"

"L!"

"What does it spell!?"

"Kil!"

"What does it spell!?"

"Kil!"

"What does it spell!?"

"Kil!"

Shouting obscenities and worked into a hysterical nationalistic fervor, and with their pants hanging down, lots of Krancky Mountain cranks charged down the slopes to battle.

Gilfgilf said, "Better stay down, everybody." Slowly and deftly, he raised a white flag on a twig. It got blasted into splinters. Remembering that the people of Us traditionally wore white when going to war, he raised a violet flag and, hearing no bullet or thrown chicken, slowly stood up. "We know you guys have had it bad lately, but we come in good will. Honest."

"Eat it, outlander!"

"You dress funny, and you smell of elderberries!"

"A pox upon ye and yers, and yer little dog, too!"

"No, really," reasoned Gillfgilf. "If my men were planning to circle around your town and hit you from behind, would they be risking my life to keep you busy? Besides, I have even more reasons to hate invaders than you. Us still has an army, and Them still has its whole population. The burnt-out husk of More of Them by the Sea only has—me!" So saying, the feisty D'Wharf flashed his exclusive Country Club card, signed by noble and polite order of High King Celibate.

"It really is an honest ta gosh D'Wharf!" cried one of his would be oppressors, slapping himself silly in the face. "I've tried to get one of those cards for years. They don't give em out for anything unless you come from the right family. Talk about nose and pinkies in the air snobs!"

THE BIG KING TWERP stood on his palace steps and surveyed his multitude. No, not good enough. He climbed on his marble lion and stared with pride at the milling throng.

The armies of the Big King Twerp! 16,300 Thugs, their tattered rags waving. 6,992 Earthmen parading in their precisely identical-looking canary yellow regulation space navy jackets!

Forty-five hoodlums and greasers from the Concrete Jungle and their ape-man chaperone. Eight hundred survivors from the town of Sing-Sing, each riding a well-groomed and trained champion racing horse. He waved smugly, and they turned to climb the ramp that led out of the Fissure. Fifteen minutes later, when they were all gone, he hummed happily to himself and clapped his hands, activating his voice recorder. "Ish, the time has come. Bring on the Twerps."

***

CHAPTER TWENTY-ONE

ON MONDAY, MAY 17, Genghis Twerp sat on a grassy knoll two miles North of the Mole Hills and bitched to Gilfgilf like a valley girl about what a hard life it was.

Extracts from the forthcoming *Genghis Twerp: His Life and Battles, by one Gilfgilf, Late a dilettante of the sea-city, with notes, commentary, and exclusive interviews with the Protagonist:*

"'I tell you, it's hard,' Genghis Twerp said. 'I spend weeks talking to these different tribes. Two weeks, by Crod! Two weeks! None of them know their head from a horse's patoot. And what do I get for it? What? What!? They question my motives. They say I'm leading them to battle and death for nothing.'

'Well, Mr. Genghis Twerp, sir,' said I, 'You must admit that you did a little of that in your youth.'

'They call me power hungry. They even call me a liar, even! I'll tell you, I was madder than ravens when my men and I came running into Us and those big bananas tried to pick me off.'

'Look at this side of it, sir' I said. 'I'd just gone to a lot of trouble convincing them that all those Steppers and forest robbers with funny accents wanted was to help them defend Santa Claus approved hearth and home and not conquer it. Then this crazy bunch of pant-less screaming people throwing rocks comes charging town. If I'd been them, I'd have potted a few of their heads off, too.'

'That's your fault, dip wit. You should have told them we were coming.'

'How was I to know you'd get back so soon?! We don't run that fast in my hometown. Mr. Genghis Twerp' said I, 'I do indeed come from More of Them by the Sea, but I cannot help it.' I meant this as a light pleasantry, to smooth things over. But, however that might be, he seized the phrase "Come From More Of" and, rebounding with his usual lightning wit, sallied forth.

'That, Sir, is what I find a very great many of your countrymen cannot help.' I took this to be a slide on the fact that my countrymen were all dead, and we fell to arguing again.'"

STILL, GILFGILF'S AND GENGHIS Twerp's disagreements notwithstanding, they had accomplished their aims. Low Stepper and High Stepper, Green Forest Folk, and Mountain Folk, Gilfgilf and Genghis Twerp all were gathered under one banner to fight for their mutual freedom and to avoid each other from then on.

They were, all told, some thirty thousand strong. Now they had grouped near the Mole Hills to see what additional support they could whip up (reasoning that the people there would take a substantial army more seriously than they had a single, mighty thewed, lone adventurer).

Genghis Twerp had found to his disgruntlement that his great personality, plus an occasional dose of forest ciggies and Calvinist wheat sauce, were poor substitutes for the Donklings' daily near-fatal overdose of dex at building a firmly organized fighting unit. Indeed, sometimes he could almost feel a grain of sympathy for the Big King Twerp in his desire to repress the individuality of all these quarreling messed up bastards. Gilfgilf ignored his valley girlish grumbling and dreamily thought about Shanie Lola McBrideburgh's many virtues.

A thousand heavily armed scouts of all the races, led by Bill Firmly and Carl Sinckmark of the Us-Them coalition (a politic move, since their men formed more than a third of Genghis Twerp's army) scouted the Mole Hills for hill-men to conscript into the Freedom Fighters.

"Ye knoo, Shanie Lola McBrideburgh, that aye find ye mickel t' my likin," said Molo, trying his best not to look too foolish from his lustful wheezing.

"Oh, Moldo MacTavish, how do I know ye're noot just sayin' that?" Shanie Lola McBrideburgh batted her eyes for emphasis. "Besides, me heart is torn betwain thee and the feisty D'Wharf."

"Gilfgilf, is it? I'll kill him, then! Would that convince ye of mooey love fair yawn?"

"Nay, it wawld fain have the aither affect. Fair I like the lettle fellow, and wawld want to keep him on as a chum even if I accept ye're endoursments for thyself and accept your hand in mairrrage."

Moldo MacTavish scrunched up his ape-like face. "Whoo said anything about marriage?"

Suddenly, the hill-fellas, who had been watching all of these proceedings with moribund amusement, and awaited the proper opportunity to surround this large contingent and wipe them out, yelled, "Look out or you'll be in for it! The enemies from the East are attacking, Mein Herrs, and there are millions and millions of them. Time to put your lack of perspicacity to test!"

The thousand Freedom Fighters at this sudden noise instantly formed themselves into a circle and each of them fired a bullet in the nearest direction. A dozen hill-men fell dead from behind various rocks. The rest of them, eight hundred strong, came out with their hands up, except for the two thousand others who were still hiding behind other rocks.

"Now, what was that you were saying?" asked Sinckmark, absentmindedly scratching his protruding Adam's apple, plucking at an occasional hair.

"The enemy are coming to wipe you out, Mein Herr. See them over the horizon?"

"They are coming!" said Medium-Sized Jamie of the naturally pessimistic Green Forest Folk Brotherhood. "We are doomed! Doomed! Yaggh! Gah! We are doomed! Aaaiiieee!"

"We didn't think they would come so fast," Bill Firmly said, firmly. "Still, as these hills let a man see things some thirty-eight miles distant, and since those armies are such a gray speck on the farthest horizon, I judge them to be still some three days off."

"It comes down to *diss*," said Carl. "Do you hill-poys join mitt us in der big fight or do you hold off? Kerplunk."

"Diablo no, we won't go, Senor. You men hayv a lot of gall to thenk you can hav a beeg shoot-out on our turf. Go fyate somewhere else. Comprendo?" And two thousand guns pointed out from behind as many rocks.

The Freedom Fighters went back to join their main army, and after five minutes of debate, ten thousand of them strode back up the hill and posted a sign where anyone who could read, could read it: *This is as good a place to set up a defense as any, so you hill-jerks can join us or go somewhere else. The Boys.*

It was a tough, grueling three days. They had relatively little trouble from the hill guys except for an occasional sniping volley. But even the number of those slacked off when Genghis Twerp instituted his policy that for every pair of Freedom Fighter picked off, they would hunt out and run through one of the hill inhabitants.

Slowly, the armies of the Big King Twerp drew nigher. The Freedom Fighters made their camp in the higher Mole Hills and waited and grumbled a lot.

Shanie Lola McBrideburgh warmed her Catholic thighs around a roaring campfire. Gilfgilf and Moldo MacTavish sat on opposite sides of her and looked alternately at her with liking lust and at each other with hatred and jealousy.

Shanie Lola McBrideburgh, sensing discord, said, "Awr'll tell ye a story aboot my High-Stepping childhood. Me mayther, Saint Christopher rest her soul," and she crossed her knees, "used to perform in a dance hall. After worak, manny a handsome young man used to stop by her dressin' room t' make bonny passionate proposals. She had a harrd time decidin' what to do about it. And she was noht half so cute nor so well equipped as aye." The point eluded her two male buddies, who continued to glare at one another like rabid weasels.

Elsewhere stood there a religious dispute between several High Steppers, Low Steppers, and people of the Krancky Mountains, the latter of whom were all born agnostics and scored with invective the religions of both tribes. "Uhh, Protestants are full of it. But Catholics, they can't hardly see straight," said a Kranck.

"Go to Hell," said a Low Stepper. "In fact, I see that ye air one of those chosen at the beginning of the universe to do so."

"Ahh, ye joostification trhoo good wairks people make me sick," a High Stepper gibed, gesticulating wildly. "Wee have faith in air holy Rosary. It will bring us through."

The men of Them found common ground with those of the Green Forest, for both had a fondness for long pine-wood staffs and a good well-made toothpick. Many tense hours before the big battle got passed by "bang the staff" matches, in which a Themsman would club his pine stick against a Green Forest Folk's staff until one of them fell over from sheer exhaustion. Medium-Sized Jamie won many of these matches.

Krancks paced and skulked through most of the encampment, trying to make trouble. Unlike the equally individualistic Thugs, Krancks hated even the physical proximity of other breathing and flatulent creatures.

On the night of the 19th, everyone slept but fitfully. People of varying tribes often challenged each other and threatened to blow each other's brains off until they identified themselves. The Freedom Fighters were all under orders to make as little noise as possible, for the enemy were only two miles off like a great, gray tide.

Dawn hearkened. Gilfgilf, sleeping by himself on a bed of rude moss, heard the armies of the Big King Twerp resume their march. They would be climbing the earliest Mole Hill in something under two hours.

"G.T., it's time," he said, shaking the big-pecced barbarian who alone among his company slept like a log.

"Myrtle, your sisters are too much, huh? Oh, it's you, Gulfy."

"You've got to get the troops in their proper fighting formations, Chief," mildly admonished Gilfgilf." And then, when the enemy targets come into range, you've got to give them a ringing denunciation after we've fired our first volley."

"Can't you take care of that stuff? A man can't lead his legions to war without a full night's restful sleep, by Crod."

"You've gotta do it. You want to keep the respect of your men? There's hundreds of power-hungry individualists ready to grab command the first time you mess up."

"I guess you're right." Stretching his limber limbs, Genghis Twerp lumbered about the camp, bellowing orders, slapping backsides, and stretching his mighty thews.

By mid-morning, the enemy marched into range.

"One volley when I signal, men," Genghis Twerp whispered, loud enough to wake the dead, though the Western armies, marching along happily, amazingly seemed still not to suspect that the Hills were alive and had eyes and lived down the lane and were heavily inhabited.

"Fire!"

Blue smoke shunted down the hillside! When it had subsided, several of the mightily surprised enemy lay dead and wounded below them.

A tall, bulking frame rose on the highest hill-top. *"I am Genghis Twerp,"* it boomed. "Only I have the power to flinch your leader's plans, but I can do it right well." He flexed his mighty biceps for full barbaric emphasis. "Return now to Antwerp and tell him that there can be no war; for if there is war, you must all...die! Like unto the veriest dogs!"

Yelping and wailing as banshees do, the Westerners charged up the hills.

"Kreegah! Kreegah bundulo!"

"By very gosh!" gasped a Green Forest Folk. "The front ranks of them be Twerps! Now we are surely undone."

The Twerps poured upwards. Short, gray, and mostly bald, nearly mindless, they were known and feared across the continent for their total devotion to any cause that came along, no matter how dire, no matter how hopeless, no matter how downright bat guano crazy.

The lower hills were guarded by Green Forest Folk bowmen, which helped explain their pessimism. Unable to even deter the Twerps by their oft-repeated arrow volleys, the Green Forest Folk broke and ran.

The second set of hills were held by gunmen from Us. These buckshot buckaroos took somewhat greater toll of the Twerps, though the Users had to take care not to pick off fleeing Green Forest Folk. The Twerps, their ranks slightly lessened, ran through and past the Us men, paying them no heed.

Since the Us gunners seemed temporarily unthreatened, the Green Forest Folk bowers decided to stop and stay with them for a while. But then, the next flank of the invading forces appeared. "A chance for revenge, men," growled Bill Firmly firmly. "The Bip-Citters are coming!"

The men of Earth, hideously overloaded this morning with a double dose of the emergency *blue* dex, fired their more than six thousand pistols. Fortunately, the killer mist in their minds made it difficult for them even to hit the barn, so most of them failed. But Users and bowers began to fall. The hill-entrenched defenders returned the volley as best they could.

The sounds of this shoot-out rang on for quite a while. Meanwhile, the running Twerps were met by Themers, brandishing their bitter staffs. But they ducked under them and ran on uncaring, for their orders were to seek out Genghis Twerp himself and tear him into little itsy bitsy pieces.

The Thugs were little fond of guns, so they detoured around the powder-fight below and trudged on until they encountered the men of Them. Staffs were more to the Thugs' liking; hauling out their thick oaken clubs they began to pound it on.

"Come on, Genghis. You have to lead the Steppers into battle. Put on your armor."

"Aww, heck," Genghis Twerp stalled. "A leader, no matter how mighty and well buffed, cannot endanger himself."

"Did I tell you about that conversation I heard last night? 'We've gotta overthrow that G. Twerp fella,' they said. 'He doesn't do enough.'"

"Who said that? By Crod, I'll kill them."

"The lead officers of each of the nations, at an informal staff meeting, catered by lizard men from a vast swamp off the eastern edges of the map."

"Maybe I'd better get suited up, then. Can you snap that thing in back?"

Taking advantage of a momentary break in the shooting, the Sing-Singers charged. Cavalry! The eight hundred finest surviving horsemen on the planet. They were led by the First Mate, an expert horseman.

Bip-Citter and Usman alike bit dirt until these legions galloped by; then resumed the shooting at each other.

Thugs and Themites also stood aside for these stallion-spur-ring speedsters. They clopped swiftly on to the fourth hill-copse. It stood entirely empty.

Three hundred yards away, past the base of these hills, two-score smart-ass looking Krancks stood sticking their tongues out at them. "We'll show them who's boss!" shouted the First Mate, blowing his bugle. Striking forth steadfastly, the Sing-Singers sped into the thousand mines which the Krancks had so busily wired.

Genghis Twerp eyed his Steppers sternly. "Better practice swinging those shillelaghs, men."

"Aye am noot a man, Genghis Twerp." Shanie Lola McBrideburgh hiked up her skirt to show off a lithe, alabaster thigh for emphasis.

"I see that, Shanie Lola McBrideburgh, by Crod. Anyway, if the sounds of battle beneath mean anything, the killing invaders should soon reach this, the fifth and final copse of hills before the River Grunjy."He paused, cocking his horn-helmeted head. "Speaking of which, are the thousand rafts ready to take off up-river in case things don't go right?"

Genghis Twerp thought with some consternation about having to go into battle himself. Never—well, hardly ever—in the many disastrous missions he had led had he had to do that. Darn that thoroughgoing perfectionist Gilfgilf; Frank would never have made him do such a thing.

He felt a tap on his shoulder.

"Hey." It was Frank. And his nose had healed quite nicely.

"Frank? I thought sure you were dead."

"I thought I was goner for a while, too. Fortunately, you missed."

Overjoyed to meet his old friend again, Genghis Twerp noticed the mad, hardly winded horde of gray Twerps pour over the hill.

"I guess it's about that time," Genghis Twerp barked. "Kick

the trash out of them, persons, by Crod!"

So it came about that the equally vicious Low Steppers and Twerps and High Steppers swarmed about each other.

Bunt! Clud. Crack! Smash. Crash. Tinkle, tinkle. It was a knee to gut, knife to neck, spear through the sternum warfare. Both Fissure-fel and Steppesmen began to bleed. And wobble. And fall down.

Meanwhile, the Users and the Green Forest Folk were forced to concede the superior fire-power of those from Bip-Citty. Leaving a thousand of their dead behind them, they backed up swiftly, firing an occasional salvo to slow the near mindless advance of the Bip-Citters.

The Thugs, at this time, were getting the better of the Them shepherds. Their adeptness with their thwackety thwack thwack staffs was counter-balanced by the Thugs' bigger, far more robust bulk. Also, the Thugs had them outnumbered.

Then an untoward thing happened. The Thugs, whose attention span rarely ran as long as twenty minutes, lost interest in what they were doing and began to wander off the battlefield in search of more meanderings, for they were indeed, as a race, meandherthals.

The Steppers were hurting, too. Genghis Twerp could put up one mean fight when he had to, and he accounted for many Twerps by first tripping them with his mighty thewed legs, and them putting them out of their misery with his trusty Colt .45.

Many Steppesmen, abandoning their shillelaghs, started cuffing their foemen with their brawny fists, hardened elbows, and knobby knees.

But the Twerps were all over them. The short, stocky bastards knew every trick, dirty or otherwise, in the book. And they were mean. Very mean. Psycho ex-girlfriend that you went to college with mean. You could hardly beat one off, with a stick or...otherwise. In fact, several Steppers *tried* to beat one off with a rather stout stick and failed.

Moldo MacTavish had so far cut eight of their heads off with his sharpened masterwork short sword. Frank, somewhat taken aback at being encompassed in a battle as soon as he, hearing rumors of Genghis Twerp's present whereabouts, had managed to trudge up several flights of hills, was as good at kicking and biting as your better than average Twerp. But several Twerps took a disliking to him, and he went down in a biting, kicking hunched heap.

Suddenly, it finally occurred to the Twerps which of their enemies Genghis Twerp was. A thousand, five hundred of them began to converge on him all at once, like a bunch of rabid collectible card gamers with no discernible lives or respect for anyone else pouncing upon someone opening up a fresh pack of purchased Magic cards in a comic book shop. It was at this tense moment that several hundred maddened Thugs strolled onto the Stepper-Twerp battlefield. They were annoyed at the constant presence of battle wherever they ambled when they all wanted just to sit down in the sun and relax. They clubbed anyone they bumped into, without prejudicial regard to the side they were on for to them it truly did not matter.

Some hundreds of Thugs also began intercepting the shoot-out of the Users with the Citters. They stood between the two sides—for their leather thick hides were rarely disturbed by shooting until they were hit and welted by the third or fourth bullet—throwing their clubs at, and cracking the skulls of, anyone who annoyed them; more often an Earthman than a bowman, whom they found pasty and sickly looking. (Ugh!)

Genghis Twerp, ever the master of strategy, sensed that his side was getting wiped out and they had better retreat. He hollered, "Gilfgilf! Blow the horn of retreat, for this battle's at an ending. Lo, it stands decreed!"

The horn blew out loudly. All the surviving, ambulatory

members of the Freedom Fighters who could extricate themselves from their current tangles, were more than happy to retreat. Within ten minutes, virtually all of them crouched upon the aforementioned rafts, rowing fast.

"Uhh," groaned Genghis Twerp, his massive shoulders sagging. "Gilfgilf, you said you had a contingency plan for total, abject defeat. What was it?"

"Weird Marsh, G.T.," said Gilfgilf, managing a knowing smile, minus a freshly lost tooth. "You'll love it."

***

CHAPTER TWENTY-TWO

"ALL IN ALL, I should say, an admirable rout. But you could have turned it into an outright victory if not for those frigging Thugs. I recommend stern disciplinary action. Immediately, if not sooner!" So said the Big King Twerp, talking by phone to the Captain, who, with Ish, shared command of the Big King Twerp's armies.

"I'd love to discipline them, believe me, Your Mass Entropy," the Captain rejoined. "But the little darlings seldom seem to understand no matter how much I pout or stamp my little feet."

Ish trooped about the Mole Hills surveying casualties. Best off were the Thugs; hardly a one had fallen, never to rise. Worst off were the Sing-Singers; only sixty of the horsemen remained, with their prancing steeds. Heinlein joined him, carrying a mess of dog tags and wearing what appeared to be a necklace made out of ears. Ish refrained from mentioning anything about it, despite his natural curiosity.

"Too bad about the First Mate," Heinlein whispered. "I hear he was a real good guy. But he never talked much. And he was pretty much nondescript, too. Too bad ya don't get a chance to know them guys better."

"Yeah, I know," said Ish.

Four hundred Twerps had fallen, and three hundred Earthers. Surprisingly, few wounded lay about; the Earthmen, crazed by drugs, and the Twerps, crazed by nature, had either avoided the fighting altogether or fought until they got killed.

Some two thousand of the enemy lay slain; not by any means a hefty chunk of their total forces, but enough to let them know they'd been worked over a great deal. Ish also discovered that two thousand five hundred of the Mole Hills' inhabitants, caught in the crossfire, lay sprawled dead across various parts of the battlefield.

"Too bad about them," Lieutenant Jedrey Spett said. "Neutral indigenous populations have their right to survival." Lieutenant Jedrey Spett had been perusing a book on military ethics, recently loaned him by the ship's Chaplain. The spine hadn't been cracked, it was in such pristine condition, near mint even.

Those of the Concrete Jungle had apparently not performed their part in the strategy, for the River Grunjy had not been dammed to prevent the enemy from escaping. But the jungle people looked happy and were in possession of a great many new silver bracelets and the odd titanium nose stud or two.

Security Chief Alf Simpson was a bitter man. He leaned on his bitter wooden leg and talked sentimentally about the old days when he had sway and influence. "Ya know, Harv, somewheres along the line we both got screwed." Harvey, as was his wont since that day in the palace when he received his demotion, answered not but merely dully nodded.

The happy army took time out for lunch. But no time was to be lost, so, even as they munched sod-burgers, Ish and the Captain and Lieutenant Jedrey Spett and Heinlein and the Big King Twerp, via his telephone from the Antwerp palace, held a what to do next conference.

"What should we do next?" asked Ish, scratching his head. "Track down Genghis Twerp's army and obliterate it, or just ignore them and march across Part of Upper Uranus conquering village after village after village after village, and so on?"

"Track down the army," soothingly explained Big King Twerp, "and slay them every one, by Crod. Spare no prisoners. Especially give the sure, horrible death to that motherless, slope-browed, fat ear lobed, swine Genghis Twerp; for I cannot rest at night until he—Dies! DIES LIKE A VERY DOG!!!"

"Okay, how do we find out where they went, then?" Heinlein queried.

"Do you have any prisoners?" asked Big King Twerp.

"One, I think," said Ish, matter-of-factly. " Rather buxom lass from the Steppes."

"High or Low?"

"She appears to be High," said Ish, making a pfffft-like sound afterward.

"Torture her," said Big King Twerp. "Torment her, give her Pain (and please note that I said that with a capital 'P' for added emphasis, mind you...) until she tells you rightly and true where Genghis Twerp's rag tag army went."

"Aye'll noot tell ye nary a worhd. Nair will I talk," said Shanie Lola McBrideburgh, who had just been brought in by two especially ugly Thugs.

"Okay, fellows, work her over," commanded Big King Twerp.

"Uhhhhhhh, no can do, Boss."

"Why on Uranus not?" asked the Big King Twerp.

"Cuz she so purty," answered the other Thug, blushing.

"Oh, for my sake!" cried Big King Twerp, throwing up his hands for added emphasis. "Send in a Twerp to do it, then!"

"Okey, dokey."

And they did.

At the sight of a small gray Twerp approaching her, Shanie Lola McBrideburgh screamed, "No! I'll talk. I'll tell you everything."

"Aha!" exclaimed the Big King Twerp. "See...?"

"They made instantly for the Weird Marsh, there to put up a last stand."

"Drop your accent when you're in a hurry, huh?" Security Chief Alf Simpson picked his teeth with satisfaction.

Having obtained the requisite information, it was decided that after lunch Shanie Lola McBrideburgh would be shot, twice in the head, once in the heart, and once in the left knee for good measure. So a small detail was ordered to march her out nearby the battlefield, tie her Rubinesque self to a large stake, and then shoot her after they went back inside and had their union mandated fifteen-minute break.

Shanie Lola McBrideburgh sobbed, her virtuous person heaved as she wallowed in her despair. "Oh, Genghis Twerp," she softly said to herself, "Will I ever get the chance to feel your non-Papist rough barbaric hands upon me form? Oh, oh...OH!"

But Frank (remember him?), the fighting sloth-eyed hunchback with at least a constitution score of 18, hid out among an especially large and noxious pile of dead bodies nearby the makeshift firing range. He saw her ample body tied to the stake and thought, *I'll bet Genghis Twerp will be grateful if I brought him this luscious broad.*

He untied her from the stake.

"Who be thee, short, sloth-eyed one?"

"Shut up unless you want 'em to shoot your boom-booms off."

"Okay."

They slipped down the hillside and onto a piece of driftwood, which sped them upriver the River Grungy to their friends.

Meanwhile, the Big King Twerp's army, suspecting hanky-panky when Shanie Lola McBrideburgh disappeared, decided that it was all the more important that they strike out after Genghis Twerp's army immediately and wipe them out, especially the

Green Forest Folk, who they now all irrationally loathed and feared.

The March lasted eight days and was, for the most part, uneventful. (Unless, of course, you include that story about the three fish, the Twerp, and the box of anvils, which is absolutely hilarious, but, alas, is far too long and complicated to regale on these pages...) Along the way, Twerps entertained the Earth troops with their clever, witty sayings which they memorized since birth:

"Regarding action, our beliefs are: Attack small, spread out, isolated enemy forces first; go against large, bunched together enemy forces later.

"All commandants and rank and file of our army must refine their combat art through constant practice, march forward bravely towards assured success in the war and boldly, efficiently, absolutely, completely, uncompromisingly, and totally obliterate them.

"In agricultural production, our core mission is to refine labor power in a cleverly planned, thought-through fashion and to encourage women to do any and all farm work."

The total mastery of many Twerps over these sayings, and their rare verbalizing of anything else contributed to the terror they helped inspire in enemies and friends alike.

As they marched out of the last Mole Hills, a single large boulder rolled down on them and flattened eight Twerps. In swift retaliation, the army plastered the hills for half an hour with howitzer fire. "That should take care of those squirrel thieves," the Captain chuckled, stamping her little foot, while punching Security Chief Alf Simpson in the arm.

Capped Anthony Spaulding was depressed of late at his lack of influence on Ish, and upset by recurring dreams that he was evolving into a mushroom, and not an edible one, at that. He went to Security Chief Alf Simpson. "Sarge, the army is just fallin' *out of control*. We have to get' em headed back in the right way, or we'll all be *killed*. Gnoamsayen?"

"Face up to it, Capped Simpson said, grimacing as his wooden leg stubbed itself against a rock," the good ole days are over. We ain't got no power to chang e nothin'. Me, I'll just settle for killiin' as meny of the enemy as come in sight, and get my pleasuer from that.

"But Sarge, I got a *plan*."

"Will it work?"

"Don't they always?"

ON THE FIFTH DAY of the march, the army arrived at the Pompous.

"Point of order," Ish phoned. "Do we take time out to conquer the Pompous, or just march right on to the Marsh? Huh? What'll it be, Your Mass Entropy, huh, huh, what, what?"

"Take the Pompous if you like, conscript as many of the inhabitants as possible. Kill the rest. Raze their culture. Shoot their cats for the sheer fun of it. Provided that the operation doesn't hold you up for more than two hours, knock yourselves out."

The Big King Twerp was hesitant to put down the phone. Time dragged to a crawl in the palace without Ish to keep him company. He'd never have sent him were it not that he was the only one he could trust to keep the entire operation from completely messing up. Now the Big King Twerp played a lonely game of chess with himself and, gosh darn it!, he always won. Thinking of future glories, which will be even more glorious than the glories he was glorying in now in his glory, he went to his secret tower library and pulled out the favorite of his books that didn't have any pictures in it, the one that told the story about a goat and a bear.

THE PEOPLE OF THE Pompous were all over 73 years old, served by a single youthful servant who had to run like bejeebers to keep up with all their requests, inane or otherwise. These peace-loving elderly people reclined now on the big front porch of their hotel—the largest front porch in anyone's memory in recent times, that could accommodate the entire population with ease.

"Ah do declare, ah will surely have a sip of peppermint flavored wine, sonny boy," said one of the Pompous's most respected citizens, an 89-year-old man in a vanilla ice cream suit, green polka dot bow tie, and a broad-brimmed white hat with dark yellow stripes. (And he felt quite dapper, too!)

"You are going to have to improve yoh rate of propulsion, boah, for yo took what ah calculate to be twenty-nine seconds just to run up three flights of stairs, open up the liqueur cabinet, fetch out mah favorit wahn, chill it and return it to me without a single drop sullied or spilled."

"Big Running Mickey Mantle Thunder Crow, sorry to disappoint you, rich man. In his youth, when Big Running Mickey Mantle Thunder Crow lived one with nature and hunted plains oxen with his teeth, Big Running Mickey Mantle Thunder Crow was faster. Quite faster."

"Do not qualifah mah criticisms, boy. If yoh insolence is repeated, ah shall have to commend a full report of yoh activities to the Patriarch of this heah plantation."

"As you say, rich man. Your straightness of tongue is known to all who do business with you."

"Ah will take that as a compliment and let it go, sonny. Now run along with you for, if ah am not much mistaken, there are othuh people on this porch requiring yoh services."

Big Running Mickey Mantle Thunder Crow ran to do their bidding, though not without disgruntlement. He judged that for all the work he was doing, he should be making more than a bare minimum wage. And souring the entire operation more was the fact that the Pompous were lousy tippers, even that.

"Say thauh, Myrtle, is that not an army advancing?"

154

"I do not see nothing, Slim."

A jolly 75-year-old man with a long white beard laughed, "You are sufferin from illusions of the eye, Slim. Remands me of this young fool ah met near the Mole Hills who told me a long made up storah about invaders from outuh space. Now ah, for one, call that poppyc—"

And at that, the shelling of the Pompous began.

"Ah do deklayuh. I think that we ahh under attack. Running Bayuh or whatevuh yo name is, could you run out thayuh and see who ahh attacker is?"

"Me do that pronto."

The Patriarch of the Plantation, a man of some venerable hundred and thirty-one Autumns, leaned out his attic window and yelled, "Are those Northern barbarians at it again? If it isn't Alexander Twerp, it's his great-grandson, Genghis Twerp. Matilda, fetch ye old blunderbuss out of the basement and prepare to muster a last-ditch defense."

Big Running Mickey Mantle Thunder Crow ran up to the howitzers and said, "Got plenty important message for your chief officer. Show me to him and snake spirit not rain on you."

Sam Bodash, manning a howitzer, said, "I don't know who this guy thinks he is, but he's got guts. Moxie even."

Big Running Mickey Mantle Thunder Crow got shown to the Big King Twerp's chief officers, and they were shocked by how rudely his clothes clashed, a true Australian fashion designer's ultimate fashion nihgtmare. But he canceled their stylish thoughts by saying, "My employers are fools, but they be harmless fools, most of them even toothless, truth be told. They are no use to you, real or imagined. Pass them by unlaundered and I will show you a quick, easy route to Weird Marsh."

The logic of this seemed so simple and yet compelling (and Big Running Mickey Mantle Thunder Crow so cute) that the Captain acceded to it.

Two days later, thanks to Big Running Mickey Mantle Thunder Crow's swift, accurate guidance, the armies of the Big King Twerp had grown close to the Weird Marsh.

Brad McKray and Joel McKray, as they marched along, and during meals, played a running game of handball. As the ball sailed up in the air, and missed, Joel McKray said, "Look over there, Brad McKray. It is Benji Silverbeaster. Wasn't he the guy who passed into a catatonic stupor but later returned to the real world?"

"The coma kid?"

"Yeah."

"Beats me. Who cares? Why?"

"Oh. I was just wondering."

But Joel McKray remained curious about this. Later, he accosted Heinlein, and pointing at the same person, asked, "Wasn't he the guy that etcetera, you know?"

"You know, that's a pretty good question, Joel McKray," said Heinlein. "It's hard keeping track of all 6,700 of our guys. Could be him, though."

Benji Silverbeaster spun around suddenly. "Quit talking about me!! I can't stand people talking about me! I can't, I can't, I can't!"

That night, Capped Anthony Spaulding felt ready to produce the last bit of evidence to persuade Security Chief Alf Simpson to accede to his master plan. He had sat outside the Captain's tent during the early evening, holding his pocket recorder. Now he played it for Security Chief Alf Simpson in the solitude of some swaying bushes.

"Come, Helen, dear, and sit on my little knee."

"Cor blimey! Why should I, you balding creeping?"

"Oh, yes, please abuse me, abuse me—I haven't felt so good since my dear..."

"Trying ta mike me jealous, oy, talkin' bout other sweeties. Well, any man in this camp could take me if I asked 'em to. Some

156

of em look right good."

"And you think they wouldn't take *me*? Oh, Helen, I want more than that in a relationship; someone strong, forceful—"

"And you think you can get that from me, eh? Well, if it's orders you want...." (Sound of two loud slaps, followed by random grunts.) "I'll give you orders."

"You see what I mean, M'sieur? Thees is no how you say 'casual affair.' Mon Capitan is taking it very seriously, indeed."

"Ya mean that ar army is takin' orders from an eleven-year-old girl?"

"Indirectly, yes."

"Then there's only one way ta stratin thinz out—I've got to take over."

"Precisement."

"But howl I do that? The Captain's a tuffie."

"For ze fourth time, I must explain my plan. *Zees* time, forget about your lost leg and listen."

Early the next morning, the ground they marched upon began to feel mushy. Big Running Mickey Mantle Thunder Crow knelt down to the turf and put his ear to it for so long that the men nearby him began to suspect that he was dead. He rose and said, "Weird Marsh—straight ahead. Can Big Running Mickey Mantle Thunder Crow go home now?"

"Sure you can, home to the Prairie God," said a Thug. He was one of those rare Thugs who used a firearm, and he shot the scout, who fell into a pool of stagnant helium.

The Thug thought it was funny.

Big Running Mickey Mantle Thunder Crow laid there and played dead until the whole entourage had trudged by. He vowed revenge against these traitorous interlopers in his land—and thanked the bronze god for his bullet-proof undershirt.

Presently, the Big King Twerp's fighting unit pulled up in front of a large white sign sticking out of the muddy, ferny ground on two stubby white sticks:

WeiRd!! MaRSh

PoPuLatioNpOpUlATIOn

"Let's set up camp here," Ish said. "No one can possibly survive in the Weird Marsh for more than a few days. We'll starve em out, by cracky."

But the days lengthened to a week, and no armies of Genghis Twerp came out with their hands up or otherwise, nor even gave signs of life. A squadron of Twerps ran thirty miles to the point where the River Grunjy entered the Marsh; only to find hundreds of neatly parked rafts but no people. On the ninth day after they had arrived at the sign, a keen-eyed Sing-Singer spied smoke rings rising from a distant campfire. The rings were apparently in Upper Uranian smoke code. When deciphered, the message read:

"Come and get it, suckers."

When the Big King Twerp heard of this, he was enraged, which felt good because the course of this campaign had bored him as of late. He said, "Sure, march into the Weird Marsh. Oh, and don't come out until the bastards are all dead."

Wisps of Marsh gas flickered across the border, almost like laughing.

***

CHAPTER TWENTY-THREE

THE HORSES AND HEAVIER artillery could not cross into swampy ground, so they left four hundred grim and determined Twerps to guard them. (This inability to bring the howitzers troubled Ish and the Captain, but anyone else holing out in the Marsh must be similarly handicapped, they reasoned, and, for the most part, justly so.) The armies of the Big King Twerp, some thirty-eight thousand strong, stepped briskly across the border to the Weird Marsh.

The air was thick, almost hazy. The ground, now noticeably softer and wetter, made mucking sounds as people stepped on it. Ish noticed that in this soupy climate, he could only see the troops within a few yards of him.

The Big King Twerp, trying to phone Ish now that he had crossed the borders of the Marsh, could get only a steady dial tone.

Slowly, a triangle walked by. Security Chief Alf Simpson, a rigorous empiricist, had trained himself to believe anything only if he saw it with his own eyes; and then only if he hadn't had anything to drink. It was a triangle, all right, and a right one at that.

A bird flew out of a blue tree and turned into a prune and ate itself with a satisfying smacking of diamond studded lips.

A piano tuner trudged home from a hard day at the office, only to meet face to face with a walking shark, who loaned him some money. The tuner blew a whirlwind out of his mouth, which whipped up all the tea in China. The tea spilled over on an enormous, bubbling vat of emerald turkey gravy. Lord Byron was enraged. Minnie Pearl was pleased. Dan Youngblom in Pillager, Minnesota snoozed.

Frogs leaped over the barrier which forestalled them from a true attainment of their Karma cycle. Lollipops speaking in horehound pig bars drove a locomotive off the Great Wall.

An alien from outer space walked like a man. A rubber band man.

Heinlein spoke for all. "Oh, the *Weird Tales* that could be told. Let's get the fracking heck outta here."

It didn't happen. They had forgotten the direction back. They could only advance, fearfully—deeper into the Marsh.

They saw inhabitants along the way. Some were friendly and spoke to them. Others scampered away. None of them looked like any of the others. One of the friendly ones said, in a perfect Oxford accent, "How no talk we dog hold monkey grease iron cereal. Banana oil!"

Everyone was scared, though they had different ways of showing it. The Twerps repeated homilies, over and over again, in unison, such as, "We must not grow self-satisfied with any positive outcome. We should check any smugness and constantly examine our faults, just as we should bathe our faces or tidy the home daily to hold the dirt at bay."

The Thugs took to hitting one other. *Thunk! Thunk! Thunk!*

The Sing-Singers whistled, *The Camp-town race track's five miles long.*

Security Chief Alf Simpson raised his twelve shooter. "Captain, it's time for this nonsense to stop. You hau led us into one mess after another. You better get us out of this one now or som've us boys'll have to take over."

Enraged, Benji Silverbeaster ran at him with a bayonet, howling like a warthog. "Shall I kill him for you, Captain? Shall I?

Shall I? Shall I? Yes? Yes? Shall I?"

Security Chief Alf Simpson coolly shot him between the eyes and Benji Silverbeaster slogged over, dead.

"You've got a good point when you said we're in trouble," the Captain answered. "But we've got a big army and we won't solve it through panicking. Insubordination is no good, and I won't have it, do you hear?" stamping his foot on the ground and sinking it in an inch.

The people of the Weird Marsh, perhaps sensing tension, gather around the army. They are small and slanted and big and purple and bunnies and warts and hair and ducks and lions and snarphs and sholps and sheebles. Their noses blink inquisitively.

"This is working out pretty well," says Genghis Twerp, slapping Gilfgilf on the back. Gilfgilf is drooling at Shanie Lola McBrideburgh. Frank looks at Gilfgilf with jealous rage for stealing his thunder as an adviser to Genghis Twerp, who looks with some interest at Shanie Lola McBrideburgh, who looks with sympathy and concern at Moldo MacTavish, who looks with a jealous rage at Gilfgilf.

Bill Firmly said, "All they have to do is stumble another hundred yards, and we'll have them where we want them."

Genghis Twerp says, "Good. Want to help them stumble a little?"

Suddenly, Ish screamed, "Ahh! I can't take it anymore! All this responsibility, this confusing place, I'm going mad! Help!!" Perhaps he said this only to distract attention from the impending civil war among his own ranks. At any rate, a bugle was heard to blow.

"It's the enemy!" a panicked Thug screams. "Charge!"

And once a charge of Thugs and Twerps is started, it cannot be stopped. The massed armies of the Big King Twerp run right forward into the trap. Steve Jones, a lonely corporal from Earth, thinks, *Boy, we're in for it now.*

161

Three men up ahead of them are riding steeds. Big Running Mickey Mantle Thunder Crow rides a horse. A tall man in a black cape, black mask, and black mustache, rides a gryphon. A sun-bronzed giant, naked except for a loincloth, rides a pachyderm.

"Let's break into three divisions, one for each vicious-looking opponent," the Captain announces. "One, led by Jedrey and Ish, will consist mainly of Twerps with some Thugs and some Earthmen. Another, led by Heinlein, will hold the main body of Earthmen plus all the Sing-Singers. The third, put together mostly of Thugs with a scattering of others, will be led by me and my own dear Helen Strongbutter." Everyone except the hairless Twerps cocked an eyebrow at this but acceded just to see what would happen.

Unknown to the combatants, due to the strangely sudden passage of time in the Weird Marsh, it was already June 25.

The three men turned and started to gallop away. "Ford the river, men," Ish ordered, "And after them!"

Ish and the Ensign waded swiftly across, the Twerps surging behind. Ensign Harvey

Baines Woofbanger was among this company, his long dormant mind somewhat revived by these weird surroundings. Capped Anthony Spaulding also tagged along; he toyed with the idea of following Security Chief Alf Simpson but decided that he had rehearsed the plan to him often enough that Security Chief Alf Simpson would either get it right without him or foul everything despite his counsel.

They pursued the man in black on the gryphon. Even as they rounded the corner, they found themselves in a two hundred foot clearing surrounded by hundreds of leafy rubber trees. The black-garbed one galloped into the trees and raised his sword in triumph. Instantly, the Twerps were shot at from all directions by guns and shafted at by arrows. Yes, friend, perched on the ground were the gun-shooters from Us and sitting up on higher branches, the forest brotherhood, claiming their just revenge.

This was terrible for the Twerps, who were used to running at a target and shriving it, but not to being fired at from all sides. They ran around in confusion and consternation until they got hit and fell and died.

"We're up a creek, Jed," Ish said.

"You said it, cuz!" said Capped Anthony Spaulding, listening in.

"Tell them to hit dirt and crawl to that bunch of trees straight ahead," Lieutenant Jedrey Spett said calmly. Ish did, and the Twerps obeyed instantly. By this means, they got to an edge of the clearing with only 1200 casualties.

They found, when they got past the trees, that they were only rubber (the trees); that there were no more of them; and they were back in the Marsh.

"Time for Phase Two," the man on the gryphon said, carving a big "U" in the sucking ground.

Even as he spoke, the seven thousand Them shepherds appeared, their staffs in hand. The Twerps ran at them, and it was hard to see anything through the blasted flurry. But the Users were approaching now with swords and the forest men with knives.

"We're surrounded again," said Ish. "I can see this will drag on for a while."

The fight raged for hours, with neither side gaining an upper hand. Ish and Lieutenant Jedrey Spett waded into the midst of the Themsmen swinging their pistol butts, for they reasoned that the long staffs of the shepherds were less likely to prove fatal than the sharper points of their other foes. Harvey was suddenly unflaggable, storming among the Green Forest Folk like a madman, singing, "For Mom, Country and Princeton (an old Yale Anacreontic drinking song)."

The man with the "U" on his chest galloped everywhere, spurring Users, Themers, and foresters to a greater fury. Capped

Anthony Spaulding pulled a bag of squirrel-flavored oats out of his coat pocket and waved it at the gryphon who ran toward the oats only to stumble in a ditch that Capped Anthony Spaulding had cleverly planted there.

The Masked Man plummeted forward and, dying, said, "You fight gallantly, M'sieur. You are worthy of this note which I shall deliver to you. But, plead am oui; do *not* open ze note until you are inside ze Wizard's Tower, for it will dissolve and be no use to you afterward." With a smile and in silence, he died, a gallant gentleman.

The Captain's third of the army chased the big man on the pachyderm. With them, as well as the Thugs, were nearly all of the draftees from the Concrete Jungle.

Thugs loved to eat pachyderm almost as much as they hated short people. Spurred on by avarice, they had almost caught up with the big creature, which they planned to hit with their clubs until it fell over.

"Do you really think this plan of ours will lead to some good end, Helen, honey?"

"Crimer! Don't patronize me. And don't go callin' my ideas 'ours,' either! It'll work right enough. Chasin' this no good lousy bastard that brought us up without no decent allowance will lead to our complete defeat of the armies of Genghis Twerp."

The Captain giggled. "Oh! Your surety about all things is so exciting! I know this isn't the best time to ask, but after this is over, would you consider marrying me?"

"Pervert! Child molester! Micro-cephalic reprobate!"

"Well...."

Suddenly, they rounded the corner and found themselves on a jagged plateau of a high, narrow mountain. A step above them were the High Steppers, eyeing them with hatred and determination and Shanie Lola McBrideburgh and holding shillelaghs.

"I think we're up a cliff," said Brad McKray to Joel McKray, both of whom were among this contingent.

From below came the bellowing of a pachyderm. Then this was accompanied by the blowing of bag playing, heading upwards and nearer. Then the strangely fascinating sight of a thirty-foot vat slowly shoving up towards the plateau, then reaching its destination and, tipping over, so that it became almost too slippery to stand and those who drank of its contents grew groggy.

The Thugs were equal to the tasky situation, however. They charged the High Steppers and matched stout club for thin, heavy shillelagh. There were so many Thugs that there were enough to detach and meet each climbing Low Stepper, club for pipe.

The Captain said, "Oh, I'm confused. What should I do? What should I do?"

"Stay where ya are, Gertie, and prepare to meet the Low Steppers pouring up onto the plateau. That's where the big guns are comin' from." Even as Helen Strongbutter spoke, Gilfgilf and Moldo MacTavish and Frank and Genghis Twerp shoved their shoulders up to the plateau's edge.

"But what of you, Strongbaby? You aren't going to leave daddy all alone now are you dear?"

"Yu'v got a wuy with words, right enough. Yup, oy'v got to join me brethren and sistren of the Jungle for some big action on the upper plateau." She broke from the Captain's grasping grip and made it up the rocks, unnoticed, as is usually the way with a jungle stripling, by the other combatants.

Rocks are the natural habitation to these jungle kids. They feel right at home on this mountain. They know there are a lot of big rocks and boulders on the plateau above, and they plan to roll them down the cliff's rocky face, causing an avalanche and killing everyone beneath without regard to their nationhood or political persuasion.

But the kids hadn't planned on meeting an equally large

bunch who are even more at home in a mountain turf: the Krancks. The Krancks had secreted four tons of dynamite on this upper plateau for the purpose of causing this self-same fatal avalanche. The two sides faced each other, and there is sure to be a fight.

The Captain, nearly forced to tears, rallies enough to tell her Thugs what to do. "McKray. And you, the thin one. Can either of you read?"

"I can," Joel McKray says.

"Good. Read them this proclamation."

Joel McKray opened the manuscript and in his halting yet sonorous voice, read. "'Uhh, this is a message from your government.

Gentleman:

Some words for Genghis Twerp. "Look on my works, and give up."

To those of you in the armed services, whoever are loyal: Kill! Kill em men! Bang bang! Kill!'"

The shooting got heavier, and Joel McKray and Brad McKray of the Earth McKrays bit rocks.

"Hoot! This is mickel like the battl's mye grundfaither told me about," Moldo MacTavish laughed manfully, skewering a Thug with his weapon.

"Just see that you live to *have* grandchildren," quipped Genghis Twerp, also in a good humor. The mighty twerp (for thus the reader must have divined by now he truly was) cracked two Thuggish skulls by causing them to meet at a high velocity.

Gilfgilf was hard-pressed. A Thug was almost more than he, a diplomat more than a fighter (*somewhat like wily Odysseus— Da Authors*), could handle. He faced three Thugs, all angry.

Frank felt insanely, furiously, unforgivingly, angry and jealous of Gilfgilf. Since Frank had returned, Genghis had been friendly and cordial to him and glad to have him back, and stopped to have a chat now and then; but the old intimacy was gone, reserved for the more comely Gilfgilf.

Now was Frank's chance to restore things. Frank shot Gilfgilf in the back, between the shoulder blades. The swift-moving D'Wharf stumbled and rolled into a ditch.

Enraged at this act of supreme treachery, Genghis Twerp unsheathed his short sword and lopped his old friend's head off. Frank's head went bobbing and bashing down the ten-thousand-foot drop of the mountain.

But what of Heinlein's army? What's happening to the Bip-Citters?

***

CHAPTER TWENTY-FOUR

THE EARTH AND SING-SING forces pursued their former scout, who they had thought dead. Though the Sing-Sing cavalry, nearly as good at running as at jockeying, paced Big Running Mickey Mantle Thunder Crow closely, he rode relentlessly onward.

*CAPTAIN'S LOG 2076 A.D.— writ by Security Chief Alf Simpson: We ran acros the river sumtymes it was up to ar neks my wodln leg kept geting stuk in the soft squishy stuf undirneath. But we pulled arselfs acrost and on the othir sid ther wuz a wod idle carvd outa tres. I dont like no totam polz ther unamerican. In a few daz itl be the 3 hunderth anivesar birthdai of ar country and in a few das ill be in total control of tha planit Uranus if mI plan works out. Il con back hom and giv em Uranus on a sylvir plater and mabe theil make me president. So I pulled out mi M*16 and shot the crap out of the unnateral tre statuw. Gota sign off now.— A.P.S.*

AT THE SIGHT OF their God shot to sawdust, all 450,000 people of the Weird Marsh shrieked with rage and charged at the Earth battalion.

"Hey, men, they don't look friendly," Heinlein commanded. "Better retreat back across the river—quick!" The drug-crazed men, seeing hundreds of thousands of snowflake-like beings—not even one resembled another—quickly obeyed

Heinlein's suggestion and high-tailed back into the liquid. The current proved stronger than expected—for they had blundered into a minor tributary of the River Grunjy and they were carried for some distance with the current.

As they rounded the corner, they found themselves facing a large, sandy hill. "Keep running, men," Heinlein remarked. "Don't stop till you get outta the Marsh."

As Heinlein stood at the river bank, seeing that the men got out and squeezing the mud out of his boots, Security Chief Alf Simpson thought, *It's now or never.* Hauling out his Luger, he plugged the chief military officer in the small of his back. The chubby Brooklyner stumbled and rolled into a ditch.

"I'm takin ovir, men." The men shrugged and thought, Why not, we need somebody in charge.

"Haul yer buts up that hill, men. The enemy's not far behind. The hill's as good a plas ta stand 'em off as any."

Even as he spoke, some seventy thousand of the nearer Marsh inhabitants were breathing down their necks. They threw something at an Earth soldier who died instantly without a struggle.

"Make yerselves into a circle," the renewed military officer barked; "Cuz I got a feeling that they're goin' to come at us from all sides."

The men were not unconfident. Between Bip-Citters, Sing-Singers and several scattered Thugs and Twerps, they numbered nearly 7,000. They formed a large circle on the hill and fired at the approaching shapes, some of whom appeared to drop. Security Chief Alf Simpson stood in the center of the circle and barked orders.

"Kill 'em all, men. Don't take any prisoners! Show' em who's bos of this here planet." Security Chief Alf Simpson fired a salvo into the air in happy self-expression.

The enemy gathered and massed and gathered until they

blacked out all horizons. Then the triangle-round-animal cracker shaped creatures began to run around the hill in concentric circles!

This disconcerted the Bip-Citters a good deal. It was hard to hit moving targets. But they weren't just moving, they were firing! Globs of a soft, squiggly substance flew through the air, and when it connected with one of the hill defenders, he immediately keeled over dead.

Bip-Citter dialogue on Heart's Grief Hill:

"Geez. Look at those critters. There must be a million of 'em."

"Say, Henry—"

"Henry."

"You can forget about that pocket watch you owe me."

"Whaddya think about the odds on us surrendering?"

"Forget it, old buddy. Have a swig of this stuff and—it won't hurt as much."

Things looked bad. Thirty Earthmen had fallen. Then even a Thug died. This was bad for the morale of these men who had faith in the Thugs' near invulnerability.

Security Chief Alf Simpson shouted, "Hey, you, Twerps, why don't ya charge 'em and see if ya can make a break in them theer ranks that we can charge through."

This stood to the Twerps' liking: Charging was more to their tastes than just standing. The fifty of them, whooping, "Antwerp! Antwerp! Marching all the time," barreled into the swamp lovers and actually broke up the two nearest concentric circles.

This gave the hill defenders a chance to reload and prepare a better defense.

Sam Bodash thought, *These Weirdoes may think they're pretty hot stuff on this backwoods planet, but I'll bet they haven't run into real military discipline before.*

The gunmen were divided into three divisions: men

standing (these with the larger rifle and soft shell bullets), men, squeezed in between the standing ones, who were kneeling (these had mostly derringers), and men lying flat on their stomachs, pointing through whatever available space between humans, with Gatling guns. As this last was both the safest position and the most death-dealing, it was much sought after. The men decided to revolve the position every half hour. It only revolved but twice.

The Twerp diversion lasted fully twelve minutes and seriously hampered the campaign of the surrounders; for the first two concentric circles were broken and the third and two thousand outer circles could hardly have a good accuracy at hitting the Earthmen with their soft weapons.

Then the gray tide of the Twerps was drowned, and disappeared. Marsh people from the outer circles filled up the inner circle, and the attrition continued.

The men were unnerved by this constant refusal of the Marshers to attack. With their superior firepower they could have handled a charge; repulsed it even. But the Weird beasts merely ran around in circles, throwing inoffensive squishy stuff that invariably killed.

The dead defenders grew. There were a thousand dead now.

Security Chief Alf Simpson, taking a more active part in the action, directed that they pile the dead up for cover. Someone rolled up a two-foot joint and passed it around the entire hill.

All this happened very fast. The flight from the river remained fresh in the men's minds. When a man dropped, another filled in the gap. There was no checking for wounded—the Marsh weapon left no wounded. So the circle of defenders slowly backed toward the center of the hill. Now the pile of dead Earthmen was equal to that of the live ones. A dozen Thugs also remained, adding their course comments to the deafening din.

The Sing-Singers begin a chorus of "four thousand bottles of beer on the wall."

Security Chief Alf Simpson walks at will around the encampment, pulling out one of the twelve guns he carries on his shoulder and firing several volleys, chuckling with pleasure when he picks someone off.

"Saydidyouheartheoneaboutthetwosowboys.They'rewalkin galongthisbridge,seeandoneofthemsays'there'sonlytheroomforoneo fusonthisherebridge,sotheotheronepusheshimoff!ha.ha."

"I'm not sure I follow you," says Sgt. Tracy Olanahan, "But I'll defend your right to say it in any court in the land."

THERE WAS ANOTHER DISCONCERTING thing about the enemy. While the pile of Earth and Sing-Sing dead now greatly outnumbered the live ones, the enemy didn't appear to *have* a dead pile. They fell, but in the general melee, did they get up again? Or were they dragged off the field of battle to decrease Donkling morale?

Four hundred hill fighters remained. These consisted of 393 Earthers, a Thug, five Sing-Singers, and Security Chief Alf Simpson. They girded for a charge that would finish things off any minute, for they probably could not withstand a massed charge from all sides now. The ring of defenders had so constricted that the first concentric ring of Marsh beings must now run around the outer edges of the hilltop itself to hit them, and the outer rings could not reach to hit them at all. Surely this would work to the Earthers' advantage.

Then the enemy stopped circling. They stood—or sat, even!—in sedentary positions and pitched their mushy hunks of death at the defenders like ping pong balls The Earthmen returned each muck ball with two well-aimed bullets. But there weren't as *many* Earthers to pick off as there were Marshers.

There was no talk now, no singing. There was only the grim business of standing to the end. Eighty Earth soldiers remained in a severely constricted circle (no Thugs, and none of Sing-Sing). In the center of the circle stood Security Chief Alf Simpson.

We are afraid that the tension of the last hour had pushed Security Chief Alf Simpson, ever a high-strung man, over the brink. He stood on the grassy knoll laughing and chuckling and chortling over his own cool head and good planning.

"I've done it, by gosh. Only John Trawler could now mangle-ate my plans to conquer the univ—"

Even as he spoke, John Trawler materialized in front of him.

Trawler took in the dire situation at a glance. "Well, Security Chief Alf Simpson, you've really gotten our boys into a sweet pickle this time, haven't you?"

"Dirty, rotten ghost! I don't have to take no guff from no crummy, dirty ghost!"

"I'm no ghost, Herr Security Chief Alf Simpson. A Lazarus, perhaps, but as hale and hearty as you. Feel that muscle. No? Suit yourself, then."

Security Chief Alf Simpson grimaced with savage disapproval.

"Yes, I feel new powers in me now, great powers for goodness. Indeed, I may be able to bring interplanetary justice to humanity. Perhaps even to the whole universe."

"Awww, go wash yer mouth out."

"Indeed, though it is late in this battle, I believe I may be able to forestall further killing." He raised the phone (which we still wonder, is it the ONE TRUE PORTY-PHONE?) above his head and concentrated. The phone shone like a pearl; a single ray of sunlight broke through the mist.

Sixty-eight Earthmen remained alive on the battlefield, John Trawler and Security Chief Alf Simpson included.

Security Chief Alf Simpson coughed, "Hey, cut that out! You trying to screw up the battle?" John Trawler almost guffawed. "You mean it isn't 'screwed up' enough already?"

"You don't know about my secret plan. I was gonna reveal it when the enemy got it whittled down ta me and them. I got a core of deuterium which I ripped off from the ship's engine when we left it. All I gotta do is ignite it with my fingernail, and ten thousand square miles of Uranus'll blow like a cheese factory! When I threaten 'em with that they'll make me King of Uranus in a minute."

John Trawler eyed him with something between disdain and pity. "You may be lying, but I can't chance it." John Trawler whipped his phone-arm Uranusward and clenched his teeth. Did a jagged string of blue lightning streak from the phone to Security Chief Alf Simpson's pocket?

"There. Whatever's in your pocket, string, or nothing, it's harmless now."

Security Chief Alf Simpson was so mad and angry that he jammed his hand into his pocket and scratched the contents. Nothing happened.

57 Earthmen left on the battlefield.

"Now for the saving of those who remain," John Trawler said commandingly, again beginning to raise the phone spaceward.

Security Chief Alf Simpson, all his hopes and plans dashed, jumped him. They struggled bitterly for several seconds, Security Chief Alf Simpson trying at the same time to strangle John Trawler and get the phone away from him, John Trawler trying to break free.

The phone went off.

"Now you've done it."

"No, it wuz you."

The phone rolled into a mud puddle and sank, not to be re-discovered in this silicon age.

The two mortally wounded men staggered back and eyed each other with disbelief; and new-found respect.

"You know, Security Chief Alf Simpson—"

"What?"

"I oppose everything you stand for, but I admire your spirit."

"Same goes here."

They fell.

So it was that these two arch-foes died, back to back.

IN HIS PALACE AT Antwerp, the Big King Twerp wonders what the hell is pulling off. He hasn't heard a thing from his army in exactly four weeks. Since all the reporters are off in the Marsh covering the slaughter, the Big King Twerp only gets re-runs from the ALL-SEEING EYE.

Maddened, he unplugs it and running up sixteen narrow cold flights of dusty, rickety, disheveled cobweb en-strewn stone stairs, he tries for the twenty-seventh time that day to phone Ish.

The phone rings! Progress, anyway.

The gleaming face of Genghis Twerp comes in on the phone screen which the Big King Twerp has recently had installed to while away the hours. "Ish, either I have to get the picture tube adjusted, or you need a shave. You look like Genghis Twerp."

"So, my half-brother, we meet for the first time since childhood."

"No! It isn't true!! You're not my brother!!! We're not even related!!!! Ahhhhhhhhh!!!!!!!" The Big King Twerp swiftly and violently bangs the phone a thousand times against the steel table.

But Ish has prepared. The Big King Twerp has smashed so many phones this way that Ish has had this last phone made out of Krell metal, three inches thick.

"You know as well as I that we are half-brothers, parted when you were seven and I having just attained the age of five. I remember the wart above your belly button. But I was kidnapped to the Steppes proper—at your instigation, I have come to suspect—where I grew up a spirited and lusty youngster, who knew

175

how to have a good time."

"Even if, for the purposes of argument, I were to admit that your despicable and trifling lie were true, what of it? Within seconds, my army will complete its decimation of your army, and you will stand drawn and quartered until dead, dead, dead."

"Oh, yeah?" Genghis Twerp stepped back from the view screen and revealed the scanty, puny remnants of the Big King Twerp's armies, who had agreed to abject no questions asked unconditional surrender.

Angered beyond words, the Big King Twerp hung up, his disposition gloomy, his regal stomach rumbly.

The phone rang.

The Big King Twerp hummed to himself for ten minutes, hoping the phone would quit ringing, but it didn't.

Finally, he lifted the receiver.

A balding, squinty-eyed face appeared on the phone screen.

"Umm, is this the Big King Twerp's residence?"

"Yeah. What's it to ya?"

"You know, Biggie, I just don't like your attitude.

"I try all this time to establish a meaningful relationship with you, and all you do is intimidate me, brow beat me, cut me down, make niggling and meaningless small talk, and, quite candidly, aspurge my honor."

The Big King Twerp snarled, "I'll bet you swiped that phone!"

"See what I mean? How can you treat me this way? I'm your *son*, for Saturn's Sake!"

The Big King Twerp turned his head sideways and squinted at the morose young man. "There's a certain resemblance. But I have lots of peasant maids banging on the castle door claiming I fathered their son. It's one of the hazards of command. What do you want, a job reference?"

The young man's eyes started to tear up. "And the worst

thing is, you always hang up before I get a chance to answer. Every. Cotton. Picking. Time. But this time, Biggie, I am putting in the last word. Do you hear me? The. Very. Last. Word."

"Oh, why don't you go slug a turni—"

And then the phone blew up.

KRAKATOA-BOOM!

A mushroom cloud rose from the dispersed electrons of the palace. The Fissure of the Twerps collapsed in upon itself.

So endeth the two-thousand-year reign of the Twerps.

✳✳✳

CHAPTER TWENTY-FIVE

GENGHIS TWERP EMITTED A great, chesty laugh. "Wow, by Crod, I'm really happy. Really, really, *really* happy. Let's celebrate, men—and women. Today marks the first day of the stupendous self-proclaimed long reign of Genghis Twerp!"

To the delight of Genghis Twerp and Shanie Lola McBrideburgh and the intense, unwavering disapproval of Moldo MacTavish, Gilfgilf was still alive. The bullet had gone in one shoulder and out of the other, and the ditch he'd tumbled into had a bunch of wet stuff in it that helped to salve his wound. Such are the inherent peculiarities of the Weird Marsh.

Of the defeated army's three divisions, those in the forest had fared best: There were five thousand or so survivors. These included all the remaining Twerps, plus Ish, Lieutenant Jedrey Spett, Ensign Harvey Baines Woofbanger, and Capped Anthony Spaulding. When the Twerps learned that their boss in Antwerp had cashed in, they immediately quit fighting, and waited quiescently for someone else to come along and give them orders.

The mountain fight had terminated with surprising suddenness. The Krancks and the Concrete Junglers, fighting each other, had accidentally set off the TNT and blown each other all up. This resulted in one heck of a landslide, which killed every one of the Thugs, and tragically killed Nazrat, who had just made sure earlier that the bulk of his young charges had made it to safety, his honor bound duty fully fulfilled.

But his pachyderm came out of it okay.

Also fortunately missed by the falling rocks were all the Low Steppers and High Steppers, plus the Captain and Joel McKray and Brad McKray of the Earth McKays.

When there were four Earthians still standing on the hill, the Marsh-men had suddenly dispersed and left them in peace.

These four were the ship's medical officer, the ship's Chaplain, a 17-year-old boy who didn't want to go, and a Quaker. Not one of these four carried firearms or had fired a single shot in the battle, especially the Quaker, who was far too busy saving his oats.

To the surprise and delight of these, Heinlein was still alive. He had tumbled into the same ditch as Gilfgilf.

"Say, Genghis Twerp, what's this I hear about your reign starting?" announced Gilfgilf, almost as if on cue. "I thought we were fighting this war to get rid of all that?"

Genghis Twerp crossed his arms in order to give his words greater and clearer emphasis. "Gulfy, a man has to rise in the world or else he will fall for anything. I turned forty Donkling revolutions at two this afternoon. It is time for me to evolve from a playboy adventurer to a wise monarch who will unite Part of Upper Uranus under his lenient guiding hand. To make complete this switch to responsible living, I today proclaim Shanie Lola McBrideburgh...my Queen!"

Moldo MacTavish and Gilfgilf looked at each other in utter comical stupefaction. Shanie Lola McBrideburgh turned her warm brown eyes to Genghis Twerp-ward, giggling petitely.

Somewhere in the far distance Queen Rabid felt a cold intrusion upon her shadow, and she shuddered. And a lone tear streaked down her face and her ample heaving personality. She then immediately took to task.

Shortly thereafter Genghis Twerp began verbally carving up

his kingdom. "I will set up my palace in newly re-constituted More of Them by the Sea. The Twerps will leave their demolished old home and accompany me there and be my palace guard. The sun will serve them much good."

Suddenly a Green Forest Folk messenger arrived, all breathless and a bit more green than usual around the gills. "Telegram for the King: for his newly usurping excellency, Genghis Twerp."

Gilfgilf grimaced (as his war injury acted up). "I'm his most trusted adviser, gosh golly darn it. I'll take it." He quickly scanned the urgent missive. The telegram read ("Stop"s omitted. I am damn tired of hearing the funny telegram gag with all the "stops."):

My own dearest Genghis Twerp:

Better hustle your broad barbarian butt back to the Green Forest. I'm horny. Or else.

> *As ever,*
>
> *Rabid*

P.S.: Or else send that dynamite short friend of yours. R.

Gilfgilf gave weighty thought to this. "Moldo MacTavish, how'd you like to get it on with a high-action fantasy chick person? Ample bosom, amphetamine wracked, yet voluptuous like unto the fabled 21st Century Kate Upton, the whole nine yards, including the proverbial kit and kaboodle. Nice personality, too?"

Moldo MacTavish, chagrined at having lost his would-be gal friend to an unexpected and unchallengeable rival, merely shrugged, and said, "Surr, woot hev aye goht to lose, eh?"

"Cool beans. Just follow this road map to the middle of the forest. You can't miss her."

"Hoot, mon, I will!" Moldo MacTavish, regaining his spirits a bit, jigged away.

Genghis Twerp rambled on. "Within close reach of my palace will be my much-respected buddies, the High Steppers, Krancks, Users, Themers, and the Green Forest Folk. And those esteemed ones of the Weird Marsh. Gilfgilf will sit by my side as he has in the past, my most trusted adviser. Ish, I keep by my other side for, though my foe's former adviser, he is a good man in a pinch and has demonstrated his willingness to serve faithfully whoever gives him the biggest hand-out. Just a joke, son.

"I'll make a real good monarch. Real gentle. I'll lay on but few taxes, and won't pry into your personal lives, if you keep me supplied with plenty of beer and money and broa,"—he glanced over at his sharp-eyed bride—"and broad-minded policy suggestions."

"You Bip-Citters are a special matter to deal with," he told the Donklings. "You, Captain, I cannot forgive for ordering the destruction of my old chums, the Munjes. You must stand yourself exiled to frozen and all too rocky Gnorway, and get thee there hence ASAP if you can."

"Oh, poo," she said, pouting and stamping her little foot.

"The rest of you are free to stay on," Genghis Twerp said. "Serve me or accompany your Captain on her long journey to frozen and all too distant Gnorway or do something else. But don't start no revolution."

"If it's all the same, your Ghengisshipness, I'd like to stay and serve with you," said the former Ensign, Lieutenant Jedrey Spett. "I like your dynamic, mildly intrusive, but easy-going style."

"I'll do the same," said the even more former Lieutenant Harvey Baines Woofbanger, secretly thinking to himself, *Who knows, I might even work my way up to an officership.*

"Likewise," enjoined the Quaker, the medical officer, the science officer, and the 17-year-old kid who didn't want to go.

Heinlein spoke up loyally. "I don't know 'bout the rest of youse, but I goes where my Captain goes."

"Thank you," said she.

"Don't mention it," said he.

Moved, Brad McKray and Joel McKray of the Earth

McKays also vowed to follow the Captain. The Chaplain and the other one threw in, too.

Capped Anthony Spaulding flipped a nickel. "Heads." Well, perhaps the diet was better in the Northeast. "Can I come, too?"

"I hate to rush things," said new High King Genghis Twerp, "but I want the seven of you who are going on this journey out of my sight immediately. And never come back. 'Bye now."

"Wait!" suggested Big Running Mickey Mantle Thunder Crow, suddenly coming back with arms folded. "I will show them the way, and bring them there safely."

High King Genghis Twerp said, "That's not a bad idea. Here Big Running Mickey Mantle Thunder Crow, take this proclamation to my cold herring-eating Gnorwegian friends, acquainting them that they are part of my genial domain, too."

Following the sure-footed Big Running Mickey Mantle Thunder Crow, the Captain's seven started their journey. Joel McKray looked back once and saw through tear-flecked eye Ish in idle conversation with Lieutenant Jedrey Spett, and Gilfgilf perched high on a rock deep in thought.

It was a long journey, longer than any yet encountered in this tale, but Big Running Mickey Mantle Thunder Crow guided them true and well.

To pass the time, they told anecdotes. Big Running Mickey Mantle Thunder Crow had such a store of native wisdom that he must have been much older than he looked. Indeed, he had already traveled so far and wide that he could tell about things *outside* the borders of Part of Upper Uranus itself. "Me no talk about those things, though," he said. As far away as Gnorway lay, he had made the journey twice before.

The Captain stayed despondent for much of the trek. Her army was gone, her noble John Trawler was gone, her stinker Security Chief Alf Simpson was gone—worst of all, her chances of getting back to the lush fields, plains, mountains, oceans, etc., etc.,

etc. of Earth and rising further in rank in the Fleet. She cried and sniffled and kicked passing rocks with her little feet as she pouted.

Heinlein tried to console her with his limited fund of wit. "Things ain't so bad," he said.

They ate simply, off of such squirrels as Big Running Mickey Mantle Thunder Crow or the versatile Chaplain could catch.

They reached the River Grunjy after two days, and two days later had followed it to the point in which it connected with the *BIG PIT* itself; the Big Pit, which no man could see across and which none had ever plumbed the bottom of.

"Incredible!" the other Earthmen exclaimed. "The River *is* running up the pit instead of down."

"Nothing complicated about that," ejaculated the Captain, who was well-grounded in the sciences. "Every schoolboy knows that if you pour 'Helium II,' or liquid helium, inside a jar, it climbs up the sides."

Notwithstanding, Joel McKray and Heinlein stood for some time in awe, watching this miracle of nature. Brad McKray gnawed on a squirrel bone.

After a week's journey (including three and a half days walking precariously close to the yawning maw of the Big Pit) they reached the widely-heralded Wizard's Tower.

The eight weary travelers debated for some while whether or not to seek its entrance.

"No," said Brad McKray.

"Yes," said the Chaplain.

Big Running Mickey Mantle Thunder Crow, for one, stood shaking outside the Tower in superstitious fear. "Radio God, eat me," he quivered, unlike his usual serene calmness. It was finally decided that Brad McKray and the Mantle would take a stroll for a few minutes while the other six looked at the inside of the Tower.

A unique feature of the Wizard's Tower is that it stood out

of the Big Pit itself; so either the Pit had a bottom somewhere down there, or the Tower was indeed preternatural. They entered by the main entrance.

It looked sort of like the 421st floor in a lot of office buildings. Some of them had seen better on Earth. But a tough-looking two-bodied guy in a many-colored double-breasted suit coat walked in and husked them briskly to an elevator. "Since you're special guests, you'll get to see the very top floor," they told the Earthers.

The elevator opened on the face of the Wizard himself.

"I knew you were coming," the Wizard lied. He was a congenial-looking man of middle years, bald on top and gray along the edges. He filled six glasses from a tall, elegant decanter. "Have some water. It's four years old." The Chaplain abstained.

"By the way," the Wizard asked. "You were all in the War. Any of you see what happened to a tall, black-mustached reporter with a French accent?"

Capped's memory suddenly jarred, he remembered the letter in his pocket and remembered that this was the time to open it. Pulling it out and opening it, he found that the enclosed missive was in Upper Uranian, which he could make head nor tail of. "What's this say?"

"Why, let me read it, dear child," said the Wizard, resorting to an unfortunate expression which he had picked up from his Saturday morning show. He read:

"I recommend zat ze bearer of zis lettre be hired to replace me. Like me, he is French. And zere is anozer importante similarity between he and I, which will be apparent to you, Monsieur Wizzzarde, shortly after hiring him.

"U."

"His recommendation's good enough for me," the Wizard quipped. "Want the job?"

"A johb? With ze press corps? How far do your broadcasts

extend?"

"You can head off in pretty much any direction and you'll see the occasional antenna sticking out of the occasional thatched roof. I expect that we have listeners and some viewers all over Part of Upper Uranus.

Spaulding's eyes opened wide. He twirled his imaginary mustache. "And perhaps, if I do a good job as reportair, you would allow me to give ze occasional—commentary? A chance to—how you say—wield ze influence?"

The Wizard shrugged. "Let's take things one step at a time, but I don't see why not. A lot of our reporters have turned into commentators. It's the fair, balanced thing to do."

"In zat case, I expect that I will sign on—right after we talk about salary and extras."

When their Tower tour ended, the diminishing band bid Capped Anthony Spaulding a tearful farewell. He stood in the doorway for some time and gave them the biggest grin they'd ever seen upon his lopsided, battle scarred, balding face.

The seven passed the next three days without incident, until the dull afternoon when they approached a city. They knew it was a city because of the loud, raucous stereo music.

"What't the name?" asked the six travelers of their guide.

"Independence, Missouri," Big Running Mickey Mantle Thunder Crow rejoined. "It is the center of sin and degradation on Uranus."

"It's loud and obnoxious," the Captain said. Her migraine had been growing worse, and she kept having a recurring dream about leading a space armada that takes a wrong turn and sails out of the Universe. Also, she kept trying to remember something her mother told her, something important about always wearing clean underwear....

What was that way the heck deep down in the Pit? A single gleaming light in the darkness?

185

"Honestly, Captain, I don't see a thing," said Joel McKray out of his pie hole.

"Shut up, Joel McKray. And speak when spoken to." The Captain felt embarrassed at being overheard talking to herself.

"Okay," said Joel McKray, "consider my pie hole shut, Captain." Joel McCray, good as his word, shut his pie hole.

The Captain crawled to the cliff's edge and leaned, peering into the dark.

And leaned too far and fell in.

The Captain's piercing scream could be heard, descending, for some minutes. Some say you can hear it still.

The six travelers remaining stood for a long while in shock. Finally, Heinlein summed it all up:

"She was quite a man."

"Yup."

But with the Captain gone, what was the point in continuing the journey? None of them had stood sentence of exile.

"I, at any rate, must continue," said Big Running Mickey Mantle Thunder Crow, "to deliver Genghis Twerp's proclamation to Gnorway."

Heinlein said, "I say let's continue. It'll help preserve our Captain's memory. Besides, maybe we'll find our destinies along the way."

"My destiny lies somewhere nearer," the Chaplain said. "Nowhere is a man of the cloth more needed than in a planet's sin and degradation center." Embracing each of them, the Chaplain squared his shoulders and headed for Independence, Missouri. The five were much saddened to see him go for he was a just and brave man.

They continued East, Joel McKray and the other Earthmen because they idolized Heinlein and Brad McKray went along with everything because he had nothing better to do. On the fourteenth day of their journey they began to trudge upon the Vast Glass

Lands.

Heinlein always wanted to know why things were the way they were. "Why do they call these things 'glass lands'?" he asked. "I don't see nothing but soft grass and flowers."

"These *Grass Lands*," Big Running Mickey Mantle Thunder Crow replied. "Glass Lands come later."

They traveled across these vast, grass, Glass Lands for several days and nights; game was more plentiful, and the only incommodance was the occasional midnight potassium cyanide storms which pounded on their makeshift birch tent.

"Sounds like clapping," Heinlein said.

"Golf or encore?" asked Brad McKray.

"*Second* encore," replied Heinlein.

"OoooOOOooo ..." added a duly impressed Joel McKray.

But they hadn't met any inhabitants of these Lands; who Big Running Mickey Mantle Thunder Crow refused to describe further, in detail or otherwise.

On Tuesday, Joel McKray shielded his eyes, blinking. "What's that glare?"

"Shut up," Brad McKray said, but the others agreed with Joel McKray.

Big Running Mickey Mantle Thunder Crow explained, "Glass Lands ahead."

"Who is that?" queried a squinting Heinlein, pointing. "They look like apple knockers."

Two men rode up on water buffaloes. The nearer of them tipped his 32-inch white 10-gallon hat. "Preased to meet you., Gentremen. Werecome to Glass Rands."

Pulling up another water buffalo, the second man motioned, "Prease to crimb on, pardeners." Four of them did climb the buffalo's back, but Big Running Mickey Mantle Thunder Crow continued walking, as was his wont, as was his will.

Around them—forever, it seemed—stretched nothing but

slick, transparent glass. Walking on glass is hard, but if you don't like falling down, you learn, and Big Running Mickey Mantle Thunder Crow had apparently learned how to do it quite well at one time prior. He merely put one foot in front of the other and casually slid along, sometimes even allowing a sonorous humming to pass from his thin lips. Uranian water buffalo, on the other hand, have an uncanny sense of balance and locomotion upon such a treacherous, demanding, and remarkably smooth surface and make for ideal transport for the yippie-kay-yay travel set.

Their new guides, Hugeo and Munisaki, were extremely cordial and provided them with details on all the Glass Land's choice pertinent tourist spots, of which, alas, there were none.

"Please to try oul lradios, y'all," Hugeo would explain during rest breaks, while passing about certain locally brewed libations. "We make them ourselves. They are built to rast, and they even pick up Neptune."

Heinlein asked, "What do you feed your Uranian water buffalo?"

Munisaki gave off a perplexed look. "Feed them?"

At last, the Glass Lands neared their end. Big Running Mickey Mantle Thunder Crow had stayed silent and somewhat aloof through most of the glass phase, but it was even stranger that the other one hadn't talked.

The ground ahead of them read "Gnorway. The more tax you pay, the more fishand coffeewe can give you. Ya, sure, you betcha."

"No can go fulthel, honorable sils. Prease to come and visit us some time, y'all."

Joel McKray and Heinlein and Brad McKray climbed off their mount, but the other one stayed on. "No can come with you, either. I am pleased to find myself strangely at home on these dew-drenched plains."

"Well, okay then. So long, Nagochee."

"Truly it is written, truly it is so, adios."

Tipping their hats, the three men on Uranian water buffaloes rode off into the glare.

"Well, a few of us made it, anyway," said Brad McKray, clapping Joel McKray on the back. Joel McKray laughed, but Heinlein and Big Running Mickey Mantle Thunder Crow thought it somehow in bad taste.

Immediately upon crossing Gnorway's frost-strewn borders, the four intrepid travelers remaining were surprised by the sudden appearance of a big man and a short one. The big man stood taller even than Genghis Twerp, though not as massive or mighty thewed. "Sure, we don't get many visitors around here," the man said through his drooping, icicle-bestrewn hoar-frosted mustache. "My name ban is Sven Olavsson. This, my short buddy, calls himself Redcat."

The shorter man, who though three foot three inches tall, was indeed dressed like an oversized red cat, interjected, "I grew up in happy, wicked Independence, but this brain-feeble giant took a liking to me and dragged me to these Northern wastes. Don't believe what he tells you about his name. Really. *All* the males of Gnorway call themselves Sven Olavsson."

Also, as they were later to discern, all Gnorwegian women were called Olav Svensson. But the big man silenced the littler one now by holding him by his neck's scruff while he hissed and scratched wildly at the air until he grew more sedate and taciturn.

The free-wheeling Gnorwegians made the weary travelers feel as at home as one could feel in a land where members of all folk wear four parkas when sunbathing. During the years that followed, they learned several curious facts about the far Northern-esters, one of which was that their principle industry was coffee transportation, hauling it by the bale from Phol-djer's Fjord in its native state.

On an afternoon two weeks after they'd been introduced to

Gnorway and after Big Running Mickey Mantle Thunder Crow had finally gotten an appointment to deliver Genghis Twerp's proclamation on kingship to the vastly amused Gnorwegian cabinet, Big Running Mickey Mantle Thunder Crow readied himself for departure. Joel McKray wept openly on Brad McKray's shoulder, and Brad McKray, moved too with this departure of the last one who reminded them of the old days of death and conquest, wept equally back.

Heinlein, often not at a loss for words, stuck out his hand. "Well, the adventures is all over now. But there'll be lots more, I guess."

Big Running Mickey Mantle Thunder Crow smiled and walked away. He turned back once; in his eyes shone green fire.

GENGHIS TWERP REIGNED BENEFICENTLY for eight years. One night, a great chariot driven by twenty-three blue swans and a gold one with a shiny red beak, came to carry him to a far distant galaxy where his help was urgently needed in the saving of it and all of its more or less sentient inhabitants. Ish and Gilfgilf and Lieutenant Jedrey Spett and Shanie Twerp *nee* McBrideburgh set up a participatory democracy with nation-wide referendum on all vital issues and a 92-percent voter turnout.

Thirty years after the events in this tale, a once abandoned youth, now full grown to adulthood, came down out of the mountains and brought peace and joy to all Uranus.

THE END

ABOUT THE AUTHOR

ERIC M. HEIDEMAN, a librarian by profession, edits the magazine Tales of the Unanticipated, hosts the Speculations Readings Series at DreamHaven Books in Minneapolis, MN, and hosts Krushenko's, an SF-discussion space, at several regional SF cons. His fiction has appeared in Writers of the Future, Volume III, Alfred Hitchcock's Mystery Magazine, Walker's Best Mystery and Suspense Stories, 1988, and TOTU #s 9, 12, and 17. Eric is also the author of over 150 essays, articles, and reviews.

ROY C. BOOTH hails from Bemidji, MN where he manages Roy's Comics & Games (est. 1992) with his wife and three sons. He is a published author, comedian, poet, journalist, essayist, screenwriter, and internationally awarded playwright with 57 plays published (Samuel French, Heuer, et al) with 810+ productions worldwide in 30 countries in ten languages. He is also known for collaborations with R Thomas Riley, Brian Keene, William F. Wu, Axel Kohagen, and others (along with his presence on the regional convention circuit). See his entry on Wikipedia, his Facebook page, his publishers' sites, and www.amazon.com/Roy-C.-Booth/e/B00A7CVLNG/ for more.

AFTERWORD

I would like to personally thank you for buying and reading this book. Writing this novel has been and continues to be fulfilling for our authors and I hope that it is enjoyable for you to read.

Please consider taking a little extra time to help others find this book by leaving feedback where you purchased it. Your opinion about this book truly matters, both to our authors and to other readers.

If you have any questions, comments, suggestions or just want to say hi, please visit our web site on Indie Authors Press www.salgado-reyes.com and follow our publishers twitter: @Indie__Authors

~Jorge Salgado-Reyes~